THE SHOP ON MAIN

Kay Correll

First Printing, 2014

r41816

Published by ROSE QUARTZ PRESS

ISBN-13: 978-0-9904822-1-5

DEDICATION

This book is dedicated to my husband. The man who always believes in me, encourages me, and always has my back. He is the man of my dreams and I firmly believe in happily ever after—I'm living it right now.

* * * * *

ACKNOWLEDGEMENTS

I owe a debt of gratitude to a single trip to Anna Maria Island in Florida and the encouragement of a long-time writing friend. Without that trip, this book would not be in the hands of my readers. I would also like to thank MLFF, my friends who have been by my side every step of the way on our 20 year adventure.

COMFORT CROSSING ~ THE SERIES

* * * * *

Chapter One

Bella Amaud snatched her purse off the table littered with homework, breakfast dishes, and a stack of half-folded clothes. "Come on, boys. We're going to be late. Get your backpacks and let's go." She swept up the dirty dishes and placed them into the sink. Tomorrow, she'd deal with them tomorrow. Right now she needed to get the boys to their father's house, then she'd head on over to Becky Lee's. She was going to be late. Again. "I mean it. We're leaving."

"I'm here." Timmy came out of the bedroom he shared with his older brother, hopping on one foot while trying to put on his other shoe.

"Backpack?"

"Oh, yeah. I forgot." Timmy hurried back into the bedroom, and came bursting back out with Jeremy trailing behind him.

At least they both had their backpacks.

"We're always late."

Jeremy announced it as if she wasn't already aware of the fact. She'd like to blame the lateness on the boys—and they sure contributed to it—but she just hadn't found the right dance of living alone with two boys, owning her own shop, and handling life. "Get your homework off the table and into the backpacks. Jeremy, don't forget to finish up your homework at your dad's tonight."

"We should have gotten it done this afternoon. I needed your help, but you were busy with the store."

"I'm sorry. I had to deal with unloading a shipment. But your dad can help you with it."

"I wanted to play video games with Dad tonight. He got us two new games."

Of course he did. She didn't even have a video game system here at the apartment she shared with the boys.

"I'm going to see if he'll let me play video games before I finish my homework." Jeremy eyed her defiantly.

She wasn't going to get into that now. She didn't make the rules when the boys were at Rick's, though he didn't seem to have a problem with insisting on rules for the boys when they were with her.

A long sigh escaped in spite of her attempts to stifle it.

"We have to do homework before games," Timmy piped up helpfully.

"Not at Dad's house, stupid." Jeremy shot his brother an annoyed look.

"Jeremy Hardy. No name calling."

Jeremy let out his own long-suffering sigh. "Sorry."

The boys picked up their backpacks and she took one quick glance around the room, making sure they had all they needed. They walked down the stairs from the apartment over her shop. It was a nice arrangement with their living quarters over the store. Even if the apartment was small, it worked for them. The price was right—included in the rent for the shop.

She pulled the door shut and let Timmy take the key and lock the door.

Rick lived just on the edge of town so there was only time for about one hundred squabbles between the boys before they arrived. She pulled up in front of the huge, old Victorian house. The yard was immaculately groomed. Timmy had already informed her that they were having real fried chicken tonight, as opposed to the kind she made, take-out from Best Friends Diner. TheNewMrsHardy came out to the porch and waved to the boys. Rick's new wife. A great cook. Crafty. Seemed to really enjoy the boys. It could be worse. But she had to admit she was a bit jealous of the time Rick's new wife spent with the boys. Bella hated the shuffling back and forth and the nights when it wasn't her tucking the boys into bed.

The boys climbed out of the car and raced up to the front porch. "Bye, Mom." Timmy tossed the words over his shoulder.

Rick came out of the house as the boys went in.

Headed for her car. *Great.*

"You're late."

"Yep."

"I'm supposed to have the boys at six o'clock."

"Rick, you're always welcome to come pick the boys up at the apartment."

"That's way out of my way."

Of course it was. It didn't matter that driving the boys out here to Rick's house was out of her way. She knew she should say she was sorry for being late. But she wasn't. Rick could just get in his own darn car and come get them if her delivery service wasn't good enough for him.

So she remained silent.

Rick stared at her a moment, shook his head, and turned to walk away.

She watched her ex cross the yard and go into the house. The house where the boys both had their own bedrooms, TVs, video games… and let's not forget a swimming pool in the backyard. A familiar pang of… something… washed over her. It was not quite longing, not quite jealousy, just a wistfulness for a normal life where she didn't have to scramble for every penny. She didn't mind hard work. She was proud of all she'd accomplished in the last few years, but she wished she was able to provide more for her boys. Well, they didn't need all the stuff and things that Rick showered on them, but it would be nice to have a bit of extra cash to spoil them just a bit.

She sighed. It wasn't like her to feel sorry for herself, and to be honest, she didn't. She loved her adorable boys. Loved the shop. Loved the feeling of making it on her own. Things were what they were. She pulled out of the long driveway and headed over for a much needed girls' night with her friends.

* * * * *

Owen Campbell stood under the live oak tree at the edge of the yard. The lawn was teeming with children of all ages. And dogs. Lots of dogs. More dogs than he'd ever seen in one place at one time.

He stood in the shade, avoiding the humid sunshine as much as possible. He tugged at the collar of his long sleeve button-down shirt. He'd at least rolled up the sleeves, but he lusted after a pair of shorts about now instead of his neatly pressed khakis.

He hadn't known he'd be invited to a family barbecue. A big family barbecue. Two long tables lined the side of the yard and were filled with every kind of food imaginable. Twin little girls crawled in and out from under the tables. More tables were scattered around the yard and filled with people laughing, talking, and eating, along with a fair measure of spilling. The passel of dogs was helpful in that regard, not a scrap of food stayed on the ground for long.

He glanced over toward his half-brother, Jake. Owen was jealous of the easy way Jake moved through the

5

throng of family—scooping up a little girl and twirling her around, drying the tears and replacing the fallen ice cream scoop of a dark-haired little boy, grabbing a glass of lemonade for an elderly lady sitting at the head of a table.

Jake hadn't really wanted Owen to come to the barbecue, that much had been obvious when he extended the reluctant invitation. Jake's mother had insisted Owen come because she wanted to meet him.

He saw the family members glancing his way, wondering who this friend of Jake's was, and why he was here at their barbecue. Owen scuffed his loafers in the dusty soil beneath the tree. A puff of dirt covered his black leather shoes.

Oh, they'd all been nice enough to him, in an obvious you're-an-outsider kind of way. Jake had just introduced him as Owen. Nothing more. Nothing less. The family had accepted that with only the occasional curious glance his direction.

Owen studied Jake's face from a distance. He could see a resemblance to his father—their father—in Jake's face. It's what he imagined his father would have looked like if the man had ever once in his life relaxed. Jake had his father's eyes too, just like Owen.

Owen searched for other signs of himself in Jake, but saw none. No mannerisms, nothing that would make anyone think they were brothers. Jake had a larger frame but moved with athletic grace. From what Owen could tell, Jake was one of those people who always fit in, could always hold his own.

He'd only met Jake two months ago when he'd come to Comfort Crossing to find him, the brother he'd never known existed until he'd come across an old file in his father's desk mentioning a possible son in Mississippi. *Possible? What the heck did that mean?*

Owen had hired a private investigator, then later he had flown to New Orleans and rented a car to drive to this small town near the coast of Mississippi. Their first meeting had been awkward, to say the least. Jake, it seemed, had always known about their father. He wasn't much interested in having any relationship with Owen. Jake made that perfectly clear.

So here Owen was back in Comfort Crossing, trying again. Where he now found himself baking in the stifling heat on a spring day with record breaking high temperatures.

He watched while his brother talked to a woman sitting at a table, then helped her rise. She rested a hand on Jake's arm as they crossed the distance to the shade where Owen was standing.

"This is my mother, Sylvia Landry." Jake glanced at Owen with a warning look in his eyes.

Owen held out his hand. "Nice to meet you, Mrs. Landry."

The woman stared at him for a moment, then slowly reached out her hand to touch his face. It took everything in his power to keep from flinching. She might as well have slapped him. She dropped her hand to her side.

"You look so much like your father." Her voice was low with a melodious Southern drawl to it.

Owen cleared his throat. "You think so?" He didn't see it, maybe refused to see it. He wanted to be nothing like his father.

"You have his eyes, just like Jake. But you're more like him. Same build. Same chin."

The woman's eyes burned into him, scorching him with shame... his father's shame.

"I hear he passed away last year. I'm sorry for your loss."

He never knew what to answer to that remark. He'd sound like a callous jerk if he said it wasn't much of a loss, that they'd never been close. The man had never been a father, not really. But instead, as usual, he just nodded.

Jake had his arm protectively around his mother. The woman patted her son's hand. "It's okay, dear." She looked up at Owen. "Oh, and Mr. Campbell? It's not Mrs. It's just Sylvia Landry."

* * * * *

Bella parked in front of Becky Lee's cute little cottage. Jenny was already there, her sporty car parked in front of the cottage. It was time for their once-a-month meet up, not that they only saw each other once a month, but the first Monday of the month was always written in ink.

8

Bella certainly needed a dose of her friends tonight. Her life was constantly poised on the brink of chaos and she needed not only support from her friends, but also a big glass of wine. Maybe some chocolate.

She climbed out of her car and shut the driver's door. The car window slid down inside the door. *Great.* Just what she needed, another wrench thrown into her previously well-planned life. Well, it wasn't supposed to rain for a few days. There was a piece of cheery news. Maybe her brother, Gil, could help her fix the window this week. Sure, she'd just add it to her to-do list, the list she never managed to actually get through.

Jealousy towards Becky Lee's cute little paid-in-full cottage washed over her, followed quickly by guilt. What kind of person was jealous of another friend's hard work and a bit of inheritance? She'd love more space for herself and the boys. And a yard. Still, she was just darn glad to have their apartment.

The door to the cottage popped open. Jenny and Becky Lee stood in the light spilling out on the front porch.

"Izzy! You made it. Come on, we've already cracked open the wine." Becky Lee motioned her inside. Jenny had decided, the first time she'd met Bella, that Izzy was a better nickname for Isabella than Bella. So began the years of Becky Lee and Jenny calling her Izzy. It always made her feel special and accepted to hear them use the nickname.

Bella crossed the yard and climbed the porch stairs. She was just steps away from the coveted glass of wine.

Jenny plopped down on the overstuffed floral couch in Becky Lee's front room. "I'm exhausted. Remind me again why I became a teacher?" She kicked off her shoes.

"Because you love it?" Becky Lee sat down beside Jenny and poured glasses of wine for each of them.

"Thanks." Bella picked up a glass and took a sip. Ah. Yes, that's what she needed. Good wine and good friends.

"Rough day, Izz? You look a bit frazzled," Becky Lee said.

"Some of it's just the usual shop craziness. I did get time to set up a new display. You guys should see it. A teal painted armoire—it's just gorgeous—some vintage dresses that I hung in it, and couple of paintings in really old frames."

"Sounds really pretty. You have such a good eye with that." Jenny reached to the coffee table and took one of the delicious-looking canapés.

Bella had her eye on the strawberries dipped in chocolate. She reached and helped herself to one. "Becky Lee, I swear you always try to outdo us with your cooking when it's your month. I mean really, the last time it was my turn to host, at the last minute I took you guys to Magnolia Cafe. Which obviously wasn't a treat for Bec."

"Oh, I don't mind eating there. I know I work there all

the time, but I still love the food and it's kind of fun to actually be waited on there instead of serving people." Becky Lee took a canapé. "Oh, my heavenly days, this is good, if I do say so myself."

"Well, Timmy had the flu last month when it was my turn. I knew you didn't want anything to do with that." Bella remembered the round of flu she and the boys had generously shared with each other.

"No, we probably didn't." Jenny agreed.

"Besides, I always feel guilty having you to our cramped apartment over the store. I sometimes miss the days of the big house in Ashford Heights, but I sure don't miss Rick."

"Here's to getting rid of Rick." Becky Lee raised her glass. "He wasn't good enough for you, Izzy."

"No, he probably wasn't, but this struggle for every penny isn't much fun either." Bella smiled at her friends. "But, guess what. I actually saved some money this month. Savings. Imagine that."

"That's fantastic. I knew you'd make a success of the store," Jenny said.

"I *am* doing okay. Thrilled to put money in savings, but I'm just a bit overwhelmed these days."

"Bless your heart, Izz. You've got every right to feel overwhelmed. Look at all you do every day. You've got those two boys to take care of and you have the shop to run." Becky Lee said.

Bella took a sip of her wine. "I'm happy with my life. I

am. I love the store and I'm so glad that Mr. Potter gave me a break on the lease if I'd keep the commercial kitchen in the back of the store. I just don't use that area except to occasionally stash things in the fridge, or heat water for tea without having to go upstairs to the apartment. He wanted the kitchen left in case the next renter— as if I would ever leave willingly— wanted to open another restaurant there, like it was before I started leasing it."

"I know, it had been Sylvia's Grill for years. When her son, Jake, took it over, he sold it soon after. Which was too bad, because it was a great place to pop in and get something to eat. No offense to Magnolia Cafe, Bec."

"Jake's decision to sell was my good luck. It's been a great place for the store and to live."

"Jake sure just up and sold it suddenly, didn't he? Always wondered 'bout that." Becky Lee said.

"Yes, he did. I didn't understand it, because that building had been his grandparents' before his momma started Sylvia's Grill. I remember when I was a little girl, his grandmother had a bakery there and lived upstairs with his grandfather. I remember those pies she baked. They were wonderful. We always got our pies for Thanksgiving from her. I thought it was strange that the family would let it go." Jenny shrugged her shoulders.

"I think Mr. Potter felt sorry for me when Rick left us, and since the commercial kitchen space was worthless to me, Mr. Potter used it as an excuse to keep my rent so reasonable." Bella took another chocolate-covered strawberry. Surely more chocolate would help her stress level. "I'm just glad business has picked up in the last few months."

"We do seem to be getting our share of tourist traffic. It helps that those two old plantations out Richland Road converted to inns. They attract a lot of people wanting that antebellum Southern get-away," Becky Lee said.

"We're getting more people moving here and commuting to New Orleans for work, too. The school is expecting record enrollment for the next school year," Jenny said.

Bella plopped a canapé in her mouth, convincing herself that it was okay to over indulge in celebration of her shiny new savings account. "Yum, this canapé is great. I swear I'm going to learn to cook someday."

"You've been saying that ever since we had home economics together in high school," Becky Lee teased.

"Well, I got that stupid C in home ec while you got an A, of course. Then there was that time in junior high that I caught our kitchen on fire. Luckily my dad put it out before too much damage was done."

"Well, notice I never ask you to help cook in my kitchen." Becky Lee grinned.

Bella sat back in the comfortable chair, enjoying the conversation with her friends, letting the stress of the day and her annoyance with Rick wash away. The three friends had known each other since grade school days.

In high school Jenny had gone on to a prestigious private high school while Becky Lee and Bella had stayed at the public high school. They had all three remained fast friends through the years, the kind of friends you could call in the middle of the night when your husband said he was leaving you. Like Rick had done. He married his new wife—the perfect little homemaker—the day after their divorce had been final. *Seriously, who does that?*

Not to mention his new wife was a world-class cook. Her boys were always telling her what fabulous meals TheNewMrsHardy had made. Bella was glad she'd taken back her maiden name, Amaud, when she and Rick had gotten divorced. It was one of her first steps toward independence, toward control.

"So, how is Nathan doing?" Bella pulled herself away from her own problems and turned to her friend. Jenny's son had been getting into a bit of trouble ever since Jenny's husband had died about a year ago.

"I'm thinking I'll ground him for, oh say, the rest of his life." Jenny sighed. "I know he misses Joseph. I do, too. I keep hoping Nathan will settle down before he gets into any real trouble."

"I heard the sheriff brought him home from a party where there had been underage drinking." Becky Lee always knew what was going on in town. She had her whole Magnolia Cafe connection. Eventually everyone in town dropped by the cafe at one time or another and chatted with Becky Lee. She was everyone's favorite waitress, so she was always in the know.

"There are no secrets in Comfort Crossing, are there?" Jenny sighed again.

The three friends looked at each other. But no one said a word. They all knew there were some secrets in Comfort Crossing. Big secrets. The swear-you'd-keep-the-secret-until-your-dying-day type secrets. The kind of secrets the three friends had been keeping for years.

Chapter Two

Owen Campbell parked his rental car in a space on Main Street and climbed out of the car. He stretched his legs and rolled his shoulders. This trip wasn't really going much better than the last one.

He noticed there were no parking meters in this town, just lots of free parking spaces along the cobblestone street.

His stomach rumbled, reminding him of his mission—dinner. He'd spent last night in a hotel in New Orleans and had worked most of the day there. He'd decided it was silly to drive back and forth from New Orleans to Comfort Crossing and he'd made a reservation at a bed-and-breakfast in Comfort Crossing for the rest of his stay. As long as he had his computer and the internet, he could work from anywhere.

He'd missed lunch, which wasn't too unusual for him, but he was famished now. He spotted the sign for

Magnolia Cafe. It was after the dinner rush, but through their big front window he could see a handful of customers still at their tables. He'd get a bite to eat, then go on to Sweet Tea Bed and Breakfast where he'd booked a room. He smiled at the name of the B&B, such a Southern sounding name.

He entered the cafe and was greeted by a young woman with a stack of menus. "Welcome to Magnolia Cafe. One?"

"Yes, just one. Could I sit by the window, please?"

"Sure thing."

He followed the woman to a table by the window and slid into a chair. He'd be able to scope out the town outside the window while he ate. The streetlights began to flicker on, one by one, illuminating the storefronts and sidewalk.

He'd hired a private investigator when he'd found out about Jake. The photos the investigator had taken of the area hadn't done it justice. It really was a picturesque town.

A waitress bustled up to his table. "Hi, I'm Becky Lee." She plopped down a napkin roll of silverware and a glass of ice water. She was a tall, blonde woman in the maybe-in-her-thirties age bracket. Probably. Her hair was pulled back, but tendrils had broken loose and framed her face. She had just the tiniest hint of southern twang to her speech.

"Hello, Becky Lee. What do you suggest?" He hadn't

even looked at the menu.

"Everything is good here. The fried chicken. The meatloaf. Cook's got a steak soup tonight."

"I'll try the fried chicken and a side salad."

"Good choice. Anything to drink?"

"Iced tea."

"Sweet tea?"

"That would be fine."

He watched Becky Lee head back toward the kitchen. He had plans to try out all the restaurants in town and see what each one was like. He'd learned that Comfort Crossing was becoming a weekend destination these days. Plenty of antique shops, craft shops, and businesses, but just a handful of restaurants. A couple of old plantations turned into inns right outside the town. He'd been working on an idea to get Jake to trust him. He just wanted to check out the town in person before deciding.

He looked out the window, carefully noting the names on the storefronts across the street. A market, an artsy looking shop, a veterinary clinic. It looked like every building was occupied as far as he could see. It was nice to see a small town brimming with business instead of slowly dying away like so many small towns across the country.

Becky Lee came out with his dinner. "Enjoy."

"I'm sure I will."

She paused for a moment. "You just passing through?"

Ah, small towns. He'd heard small town folk always needed to know what was going on with strangers to their town. It was so different than Chicago, where no one really asked him about his business, or his life for that matter. "Here on business for a few days." That was close enough to the truth.

"Got a place to stay?"

"I was staying in New Orleans, but I'll be staying at Sweet Tea Bed and Breakfast for a while."

"The Sweet Tea. Good choice. Rebecca and Larry are the best. You're in for a real treat with her breakfasts. It's just right down the street. Can't miss it."

"Thanks."

"Well, I'll let you eat then." Becky Lee hurried away toward another table with a couple and a small boy who was standing beside the table, pulling on his father's hand, obviously ready to leave.

The fried chicken was excellent. Becky Lee's suggestion had been good. He noticed they served no alcohol here, just soft drinks, coffee, tea, and lemonade. He filed away that fact.

After he finished his meal, he pulled out the small leather notebook he always carried and jotted down a few notes. He couldn't help it. He was a perpetual note taker. It was how he kept his life in order. He liked order. He may be a bit obsessed with it, but he was sure that was a good trait.

* * * * *

Bella was too tired to think about making dinner. The boys were at Rick's and she didn't feel like being alone. She decided to head over to Magnolia Cafe because she knew Becky Lee was working tonight. It was after the dinner rush and Becky Lee would probably have time to talk while she worked. Keely, the owner of the cafe, knew she had a great worker with Becky Lee and never minded if Becky Lee chatted with the customers.

She walked down the street to the cafe. There was a hint of coolness in the late spring air. The street lights were just flickering on, throwing a charming glow to the sidewalks. She loved this town so much. She'd lived here her whole life with no desire to move anywhere else. Her parents were gone now, but her brother, Gil, had taken over the Feed and Seed that her father used to run. It seemed like neither one of them wanted to ever move away. She was glad to still have some family in Comfort Crossing. Her aunts had moved down to the coast at Bay St. Louis. She still saw them when she could—which she felt guilty wasn't more often. She shook her head. She always found more things to feel guilty about.

She entered the brightly lit restaurant and noticed that only a few tables were filled at this late hour. The Jensens and their young son, Bobby, were just leaving. She waved to them. A man she didn't recognize sat at a table by the window.

Keely motioned to her to take any table. She decided to sit at the counter so Becky Lee could work on her evening clean up chores of filling shakers and rolling napkins while they chatted. She slipped onto a stool at the counter.

Becky Lee came out from the kitchen with a tray of food balanced on her hip.

"Hey there, Izzy. I was hoping you'd stop in tonight."

Bella was glad her friend was working. She sometimes hated eating alone. Rick had ordained that Wednesday nights worked best for him to have the kids during the week and she'd agreed to it. Plus the first Monday of the month, which is why she and Becky Lee and Jenny had started their Monday night get-togethers on that day. She'd agreed to almost everything in their divorce. Rick was a hard person to fight. He was used to getting his way.

"I'll be right back." Becky Lee crossed over to a table where a couple who looked familiar was sitting. Bella knew she'd seen them around town, but didn't know them personally.

Becky Lee came back and slid behind the counter. "What are you having tonight?"

"I'll just have a salad. House dressing. Possibly a slice of pie for dessert." Bella nodded towards the front window. "So, who's the guy in the suit by the window?"

"Some guy here on business. Staying with Rebecca and Larry at the the Sweet Tea."

"We sure get a lot more people in town these last few years. It's good for business."

"It is. Keely's happy that Magnolia Cafe is doing so well these days."

"Business has picked up at the shop, too. I'm thankful for that."

"I'm proud of you, Izzy. You've worked really hard and have done it all on your own."

The stranger from the table by the window came up to the counter. A city man, from the looks of him. Tall, dark hair, and a muscular build that said gym, not hard physical labor.

"Izzy, meet... oh, I'm sorry. I didn't catch your name."

Bella had to hide a smile. Becky Lee was fishing for information.

"Owen. Owen Campbell." He turned to Bella and held out his hand to her.

She shook his hand, surprised at its warmth and strength. She didn't know why she thought he'd have a cold handshake. "Hi, Mr. Campbell."

"Call me Owen, please. Nice to meet you, Izzy." He easily just slid into using her first name. Well, using Izzy, which was what Jenny and Becky Lee called her. The rest of the world called her Bella, but she didn't mind Owen using her nickname. It had a kind of nice ring on his voice.

"I hear you're staying at the Sweet Tea. You'll enjoy it. Rebecca has done such a great job of fixing the place up. An old house, kind of a mix between Victorian and I'm not sure what. Very pretty though."

The man—Owen—smiled at her. Was it possible to have a businesslike smile? Because if so, he'd nailed it.

He turned to Becky Lee. "Do I pay you?"

"Right here at the cash register." Becky Lee moved down to the end of the counter.

Becky Lee checked Owen out at the old fashioned cash register. Becky Lee seemed to always be able to coax it to work. The man turned and waved back to Bella as he left. She wondered what he was doing in town. No telling.

"He's right cute, huh? In a city-type kind of way." Becky Lee came back and placed a salad and a piece of peach pie in front of her. "You know you want that pie, Izz."

She sighed. "Yes, I do. It never hurts to end your day with pie."

* * * * *

Owen parked in front of the Sweet Tea Bed and Breakfast, noting the immaculately groomed front yard and the wide front porch on the old Victorian-ish house. Lights from inside spilled out on the porch, illuminating wooden rockers. As he climbed the stairs to the porch he saw a wide swing at the far end. The quintessential Southern front porch.

Jake hadn't offered to let Owen stay with him, not that Owen would have accepted. He figured Jake still needed his space and time to process everything. Heck, Owen needed time to process everything. He had a brother. It still was all so new.

Before he could decide whether a person knocked at the front door of a bed-and-breakfast—he'd never stayed at one—he was met at the front door by the owners

"I'm Rebecca, and this is Larry."

A couple in their fifties, he'd guess, stood in the entryway.

"You must be Mr. Campbell."

"Please, call me Owen."

"Owen it is." Larry stepped forward. "May I take your bag for you?"

"No, that's fine. I've got it."

"Okay, I'll leave you to register with Rebecca then. She wants me to run to the market for eggs. Needs more of them for breakfast." Larry slid past him and out the door.

Owen looked around the bed and breakfast. A front room with a fireplace was decorated with a mix of comfortable furniture and a few antique pieces. Lamps were scattered around the room, making it bright even after darkness had fallen outside. It was an inviting and cheerful room that implied a person should come in and get comfortable.

"Here. Let's get you registered."

He followed Rebecca over to an old wooden counter near the entryway. He appreciated the fact that the inn had an online registration system in place. So many smaller businesses hadn't set up this step, which he considered important in this day. He'd hopped online to get directions from the website, but once he'd reached

Main Street, it was hard to miss any business on the street. He was staying at least a few days and he hoped to have lots of time to get to know Jake. His brother had agreed to meet him tomorrow for dinner. It was a start at least. Jake didn't trust him, that much was obvious. Not that Owen blamed him. Their father had pretended that Jake didn't exist, so there wasn't much to build upon.

"I made up the green room for you. It's on the front of the house, but you won't find it noisy. We have two other rooms occupied right now. I put coffee on at six. You're free to come down and grab some before breakfast."

"Sounds good. I'll be up early. I have a busy day tomorrow." He'd scheduled an online video conference for the morning, and his team was sending him a report he'd requested that he wanted to go over in the afternoon.

Rebecca smiled at him. "Well, follow me, and I'll show you to your room."

He followed the woman up the stairs and down the hallway to the end. She opened the door and stood aside for him to enter. He could see why it was named The Green Room. The walls were the palest shade of green. The room had some splashes of green in the decorating, but nothing overwhelming. A four poster bed filled just enough of the room, leaving quite a bit of space to walk around. An antique dresser was against one wall. An overstuffed chair was in front of the window with a small table and lamp next to it. A small writing desk was against the wall, a perfect work area for him.

"You've done a great job with your B&B. The downstairs is well done, and this room is perfect." He hoped he didn't sound like he was reciting the plus points of the establishment. He couldn't help himself. He was always mentally checking off what small businesses did well or did poorly.

"Thank you." Rebecca blushed with pride. "Besides enjoying running the B&B, I do love to decorate it. I'm always changing something. My Larry says he gets tired of moving things around for me and rolls his eyes when I come home with something new, but he doesn't really mind."

"You've done a great job." He'd been a bit unsure of staying in a bed-and-breakfast while he was in town. He was used to anonymity, just a person in a room, in a hotel. But if he wanted to stay in Comfort Crossing, he had no choice but to find a small motel or bed-and-breakfast for his stay. "Do you need anything else?"

"No, this is fine."

"I'll see you in the morning then."

"Yes, I'll see you then." Owen closed the door behind the woman and placed his suitcase on the luggage rack. He opened the suitcase and hung up his clothes so they wouldn't get any more wrinkled than they had during the trip here. He took his travel kit to the bathroom. The bathroom had cream walls and dark green plush towels. It was a small bathroom, but not tiny. A shower and bath combination at one end and a sink with just the right amount of counter space against the wall. Nicely done.

He walked back into the bedroom and took off his shoes. He grabbed a stack of folders from his briefcase, along with his computer. He settled back against the stack of pillows on the bed and began reading through the information in the files as well as checking the photos his assistant had sent to his tablet. Yes, he hoped his plan was going to work out well here.

Chapter Three

The next morning Owen stood on the sidewalk of Main Street in Comfort Crossing, Mississippi. He admitted it was a quaint little town with its cobblestone main street, well-kept storefronts, a park off Main Street that looked like it belonged on a postcard. There were even old fashioned street lamps lining the street.

His research team had done a good job of providing him with information that he needed to make his decision. He'd read the team's statistics and the town was having a good revival. The small town had come up with a handful of festivals throughout the year to attract tourists. More families were moving here from the New Orleans area and commuting to work.

But he wanted to see the actual building. It was a well maintained building. Large old windows, brick walls, updated electricity. The building even had a new roof. His architects had come up with a plan on how to update the building to make it a bit more efficient for the business.

Owen walked down the street, looking into the store fronts, noting the range of businesses from a handful of shops, to galleries, to professional businesses, and the shop in the building he wanted to buy. Bella's Vintage Shop. He'd been told it was a mix of antiques, decorating items, and gifts.

He opened the door to the shop to take a look at the inside of the building. A bell jangled from over the door. Nice touch. He appreciated the small details in businesses.

A woman looked up as he entered the store. "May I help you?" Her warm Southern voice welcomed him.

"I'm just wanting to browse."

"Take your time. There's also more upstairs. The stairs are in the back of the building. Call out if you need me."

"Will do."

Owen walked through the shop, noticing the displays the shop had put together. Each room was a feast to the eyes, cajoling a person to recreate the mood in their own home. Someone had a really good eye for putting things together. Unusual combinations of items. He would bet the shop did a good business.

He walked up the stairs The windows on this level looked to be originals, old glass panes with metal grids. More exposed brick walls. He was hoping they could save a lot of the original wooden floors. He walked down the stairs and back to the front of the store.

"Find anything you like?"

"Someone has done a really nice job with the shop. A good eye for color and combining unusual items together."

"Thanks. I'll let the owner know. She has a talent for setting up the displays, doesn't she?"

Bella, the owner, he presumed, since the shop was Bella's Vintage Shop.

The bell over the door jangled again and the woman turned to greet the new customers. A trio of ladies chattered their way into the shop. He watched as they picked up objects and oohed and aahed over everything.

Time to make his escape. As the woman went to show the customers how an intricately carved wooden box opened, he slipped out the door.

* * * * *

The weather was one of those perfect spring days that lured a person outside with promises of sunshine and warm breezes. Bella took a much needed afternoon off work to take the boys to the town park. She sat on a bench and watched them run around with a bunch of their friends. She figured her ex-husband owed her one for wearing the boys out before they went to his house for a long weekend. The boys didn't have school tomorrow, so Rick was taking the boys until Sunday night.

Rick had said he wanted the boys this weekend and he

was used to getting his way. It took too much energy to argue with him, so she usually gave in. She still had the boys most of the time because Rick would go out of town on business for weeks at a time fairly often.

Anyway, the acquiescing to Rick's whims was a routine she'd gotten into when they first had gotten married. That first year he had started to critique what she wore—he didn't like anything bright— and what she cooked. Rick had gotten rid of a car she loved that had been her father's, and bought a fancy one that she never liked. When she'd gotten pregnant with Jeremy, Rick had commanded she stay home with him. Their lives had always been planned around what Rick wanted, what Rick demanded.

After they separated, Rick had insisted that opening the shop was a mistake, that she'd never make a go of it. But she'd stood up to him for the first time in her life, and opened the shop anyway. It was the first time she had ever in her life tried to support herself totally on her own. It felt darn good, too.

She'd gone from living with her parents with them taking care of her and voicing their frequent decisions on her choices in life, to marrying Rick, where her decisions and ideas weren't even taken into consideration. The shop had been a heady freedom, an independence she thoroughly enjoyed.

When Rick had told her he wanted a divorce, she would have never believed her life would work out like it had. They were civil, if not friendly, with each other. The boys seemed to be adjusting to their new lives. She now had her store, which she truly loved. The living area above the store was a bit cramped for them and the boys were always bickering about sharing a room, but it was working out okay. They could walk to and from school, it was only a few blocks away.

Timmy came running over. Jeremy was right on his heels. "Mom! Throw us the soccer ball. We're going to play soccer." Timmy was out of breath from the race with his brother.

Bella leaned down to the soccer ball resting at her feet and tossed it to them. "Here you go."

"Thanks, Mom." Jeremy caught the ball with his feet and dribbled it over to the grassy area where a handful of boys had gathered.

She watched as the group of boys divided up and started their game. Laughter and shouting carried across the park. She sat watching the boys and letting her mind wander. Jenny had invited her over for dinner on Saturday. She knew her friends were always trying to keep her busy on weekends that the boys were at Rick's. Though, honestly, her life was so chaotic these days, she didn't mind a few nights alone with a book and a hot bath.

A shadow passed over her.

"Hello."

Bella looked up into the glare of the sun. She squinted

her eyes. Ah, the Owen guy. "Hi, Owen."

"Are you just sitting here enjoying this great weather?"

"Yes, well no, I'm watching my boys. They're over there playing soccer." She pointed over to the group of boys running around the field.

"Ah, I see. Which ones are yours?"

"The one in the red t-shirt and… oh, there's Jeremy. He's got the ball now."

"They must keep you busy."

"That they do."

Owen sat down on the bench with her. He was dressed more casually this time, but still more dressed up than most people in the town. He had on grey dress slacks and a button-down shirt in a pale blue color. The whole outfit, and Owen, looked like they should be in some fancy magazine.

"You have a very pretty town."

"We do."

"Have you lived here long?" Owen stretched out his long legs in front of him. He had on black leather shoes that look like they cost more than all of the shoes in her closet, combined.

"My whole life. Born and raised here."

"That must be nice to be so connected to a place."

Bella hadn't really thought of it that way, but it was nice. She liked knowing so many people in town, and recognizing most of the others. She did feel connected to Comfort Crossing and had no desire to leave. "Where are you from?"

"I live in Chicago right now. Moved around most of my life. California—the LA area, London, Houston, Philadelphia, California again. Anyway, those are just a few of the places I've lived. Don't really have a place I'd call my home town." Owen's eyes held a hint of sadness.

"That's a lot of moving around." She didn't envy him at all. She knew a lot of people would think it dreadfully boring to live in a small town, the same one where she grew up, for her whole life. She didn't care. She loved it here. The heady smell of the magnolias, the humid earthy aroma in the heat of the summer, the swishing of the willow trees in the backyard of the house she grew up in and her brother still lived in. She even liked the muggy heat of the summers. She could drink in that summer evening air with the sounds of crickets and stars chasing across the sky. She was a Southern girl through and through. Comfort Crossing would always be her home.

* * * * *

Owen looked over at the sunlight hitting the copper red hair of the woman sitting next to him. The faint breeze blew locks of it away from her face. She reached up and tucked a fly away tress behind her ear. Izzy sure lived in a different world than he did. Small town in the South. Friendly people who knew you as they passed by on the street. He wondered what that would be like. Not that he'd really ever have a chance to find out. He moved around from Chicago to one town after the next, setting up the business he took over.

She kept glancing over to watch the boys as Owen talked to her, keeping an eye on them, but not in a hovering type of way. She was just letting them have fun with their friends. Free play. He wasn't sure he ever had much of that growing up. There was always sports team practice, private music lessons, and private tutors to make sure he made the highest grades.

Izzy's boys and their friends looked like they were just having a good time. A couple of times the game devolved into a wrestling match, but they were all laughing. He wondered if she ever felt like she should step in and stop the roughhousing. It was all so foreign to him, kids playing and rolling in the grassy dirt.

He watched while the two boys came running up to their mother. The younger one had a hole in the knee of his jeans, and his shirt was untucked. The older boy sprinted ahead of his brother. They both raced up to Izzy, breathless.

"Mom, do we have time to go get ice cream?" The older boy came to a stop in front of his mother. The younger boy ran right into his back. The older boy turned to his brother. "Dork."

"Jeremy, no name calling." Izzy pinned a no-nonsense look on her son. "Can you show some manners and say hi to Mr. Campbell?"

The boy reached out his dirty hand. "Hello."

Owen paused, unsure what to do or say. He didn't

generally have conversations with the younger of the human species. "Hello." Owen took the dirty hand in his own. The small hand clasped his for just a moment then disappeared into the pocket of the boy's jeans.

The younger boy came up but didn't offer a handshake. The boy eyed him a bit suspiciously, but did as his mother had told him. "Hi, I'm Timmy."

"Hello, Tim. Nice to meet you."

They were cute kids, as kids go, with brown hair and big brown eyes. Timmy had a slash of dirt or grease across his forehead. Looking at the boys, he figured it would take Izzy at least twice through a washer to get their clothes clean.

"Mom, can we go for ice cream?" Jeremy asked again.

"No, I'm sorry. We don't have time. I need to get you boys home and cleaned up before I take you to your father's."

"Please?"

"Not today."

Izzy stood up, her red hair blowing in her face. She flipped it back away from her eyes. She turned to look directly at him and he caught his breath. He sat there looking at her green eyes. Mesmerized by them. Like someone under a spell.

"Well, it was nice talking to you Owen."

"Nice talking to you, too." Oh good, the words came out and made sense. He wasn't sure his brain was working quite right now. He'd been caught off guard by those enchanting green eyes. *And why was he thinking things like enchanting eyes?*

"Okay, come on boys. Let's go get y'all cleaned up."

Timmy grabbed his mom's hand and pulled her away, flipping a small wave in Owen's direction. Jeremy gave Owen a long look then turned away. The mother and sons walked down the pathway and out of the park.

He was surprised by the feeling of jealousy, or maybe it was longing, that slid over him. He'd never had that. A mother who took her sons to the park and let them play with their friends and get dirty. He was envious of Izzy's boys, and to be honest, envious of Izzy, too, for having that kind of family time with her boys. He could only imagine what their lives must be like. A life of hugs, handholding, days in the park. Maybe he was glamorizing it. What did he know about family life such as that?

Izzy's boys seemed like good kids. He guessed anyway. Owen freely admitted he wasn't used to kids. He hadn't been around them much. He was an only child himself, so no favorite uncle thing going on for him with nieces or nephews. Kids always made him feel out of place, like a stranger peeking into a forbidden world. A world he hadn't had as a boy. A world he probably would never have as an adult. A world that drew him in, taunted him as always—just out of reach.

He tucked away one other little detail. The boys were going to their dad's tonight. He hadn't seen a ring on

Izzy's fingers, though why he even noted that detail was beyond him. He didn't have time to date anyone. Plus, he didn't really plan on being here very long. Probably just a few more days if Jake turned him down.

He pulled out his small notebook from his pocket and jotted down the names Timmy—the younger one, and Jeremy—the older boy. For some reason he wanted to make sure he remembered Izzy's boys' names. He was pretty sure she wouldn't be pleased if he messed their names up.

* * * * *

"You don't owe me anything." Jake put down his fork and shoved his plate away.

"I didn't say I did. This is something I want to do." Owen met Jake's angry stare.

"I don't need anything from you. I don't need your father's charity. I've done just fine without it."

"This isn't charity. This is yours, pure and simple. Just because Father didn't acknowledge you, doesn't mean you aren't due an inheritance."

"Let me repeat myself. Slowly, since you didn't understand the first time. I do *not* need anything from that man."

"Okay, consider it from your brother then."

"No."

"Jake, why are you being so stubborn? I can do this for you. For your mother."

Jake paused a moment at the mention of his mother.

"No, I don't think she wants his money either. She asked for help at one time, when she found out she was pregnant. He refused and claimed I wasn't his. But, considering the man was the first person my mother ever slept with, I'm his. Not that I like to know about my mother's lovers. But I do know that one fact."

"My father was wrong. He was wrong about so many things. He was a cold-hearted jerk."

Owen sometimes thought that Jake had gotten the better deal out of life. Look at him with his big, rowdy, loving family. That was something money couldn't buy, though he was sure their father could have made Jake and his mother's lives so much easier. But Owen was sure that his father considered Jake a mistake… and his father never made mistakes. He just reinvented history and molded it to shape how he wanted it to be.

"My father and mother were… very different from your family. I had a constant string of nannies growing up. My parents were always away somewhere. I was plopped into boarding schools and summer camps."

"So you want me to feel sorry for you now?" Jake leaned back in his chair.

"No. Not at all. I'm sorry my father didn't acknowledge you, but then he barely acknowledged me. You obviously come from a big loving family."

"And I wouldn't trade them for all the money in the world."

"I don't blame you."

"But it still doesn't make it right, what your father did. My mother has struggled everyday of her life to put food on the table and clothes on my back. Her family helped where they could, but none of them had much to spare."

"I'm sorry you had to live like that."

"I swear, Owen. You are clueless. Don't feel sorry for me. I had a rich life in other ways. But your dad could have made it easier on my mother. I'm just stating that fact."

"He could have. But he didn't. Now I'm trying to make that right." Owen leaned forward. "By the way, he's *our* father, not my father."

"The man is nothing to me." Jake pushed back from the table, his meal uneaten. "I don't want anything from him, or from you."

Owen watched as his brother stalked out of the diner. Now he wasn't sure if he should proceed with his plans or not. He'd had such high hopes when he had found out about Jake. Unrealistic dreams that they'd become friends. That he'd finally have a chance at the family he'd always wanted.

He pushed back from the table, no longer hungry. He could be just as stubborn as Jake. He was going to go ahead with his plans. Jake would just have to adapt. He'd talk directly to Jake's mother. Maybe she'd be more reasonable.

Chapter Four

Bella clicked the transfer icon on her online banking screen with a flourish of pride. The money she'd finally been able to save from profits of her shop this month transferred from her checking account to her savings account. That was twice now she'd saved money. She smiled at the increased balance in savings. She was really making this happen. Her store, Bella's Vintage Shop, was not only supporting the boys and her, but was generating enough to put some cash away. She gave herself a mental high-five. Soon she'd have enough in savings to start to feel safe. For the first time in her life she'd provided her own financial security. Her life was finally sorting itself out.

She looked across from the end of the counter where she kept her laptop, to the row of windows across the front of the shop. The spring sunshine streamed through the windows and spilled across the old wooden plank floor and brick walls. She loved this old building.

It had been a few long years to get to this point, but she was so proud of herself. She'd proven her decision to open the shop had been a good one, in spite of all the people telling her it wouldn't work out. Well, one person in particular, but she didn't have to listen to his opinions anymore.

The bell over the door to the shop jangled, announcing a customer. She looked up from her work to see Mr. Potter, her landlord, enter the store.

"Mr. Potter. Good to see you." She rose from behind the counter, and came out to meet him.

Mr. Potter had been a great landlord. He'd given her a fair rental price and she'd been grateful to him for letting her rent the building without putting down the first and last month's rent as a deposit.

"Bella, I have some news. I know it's sudden, but someone has put an offer on the building. A good offer. I've decided I'm going to move to South Carolina near my brother."

Bella's heart plunged.

"I know your lease is month-by-month. I'll be sure to tell the buyer what a great tenant you've been, but I can't guarantee that they'll still rent it to you. I should know in about a week if the deal will go through, but I'm fairly confident that it will."

The euphoria of just brief moments ago mocked her.

Mr. Potter looked at her expectantly.

Bella swallowed hard, trying to squeeze out some encouraging words, unwilling to let him see her distress. "I understand. I'm sure you'll like living near family." Mr. Potter's wife had died a few years ago, and his children were scattered across the country.

"Well, my brother and I are both widowers now, and figured we'd move in together. Gets kind of lonely living alone. I'm sorry about how this might affect your business though. And, of course, your living arrangements."

"Don't worry about us, I know it's business. Maybe the new owner will let us rent from him. Or I'll look for a new place for the shop. Thanks for letting me know." Bella forced a smile, not wanting him to know what a blow this was to her carefully carved out life. Her mind whirled with thoughts. What were rentals going for now on Main Street? How would she be able to afford a new shop space and a new place to live? Why was her life always spinning out of control based on someone else's decision?

Mr. Potter turned to leave. "Bella, I'm really sorry. I know this was a shock. Like I said, I'll mention what a great tenant you've been."

"Thanks, Mr. Potter."

A month-by-month lease had always been a gamble. It was one that she'd been willing to take. She'd felt secure that Mr. Potter would continue to rent to her, month after month. She hadn't thought ahead to the reality that Mr. Potter might sell the building and move away. Bella walked back behind the counter and sat down. She stared at the computer screen informing her that her banking session had expired due to no activity. She logged back in and stared at her account balances. The meager savings account wouldn't even be enough for a deposit on a storefront, much less a deposit on a place to live.

How was that for the shortest time in history for reveling in hard-won security? It had lasted all of about ten minutes of her life. She gave herself permission to panic now.

* * * * *

Bella spent the evening at her computer, searching for a place for the shop if the new owner didn't want to rent this one to her. And a place to live. She couldn't forget she'd need to rent two places now.

She'd worked so hard for her independence, to be able to support herself and the boys. She'd done it all on her own and was darn proud of it. Her brother, Gil, had given her a small loan to open the store. He'd insisted she accept the loan, since he'd taken over the family business and always felt that half of it should be hers. But she'd slowly paid back the loan, against Gil's wishes, and was debt free now. Gil wouldn't have any money to loan her now though because he had sunk his savings into expanding the Feed and Seed and remodeling his home.

She couldn't afford much more in rent. She didn't

want to move off of Main Street with its great visibility, but she wasn't finding much available there. At least not in her price range.

Bella fought off the overwhelming thoughts of helplessness. Well, not so much helplessness—she never pictured herself as helpless. But once again her future was being determined by someone else's decision. She had worked so hard the last few years to bring order back to her life. Stability. Independence. Control.

She got up to peek in on the boys. They were both sound asleep. Timmy, as usual, was sleeping sideways on the bed. She crossed over and slid him back on the pillow and pulled up the covers. He sighed in his sleep. The moment washed over her with just how perfect her life had become and just how fragile it was now. She leaned over and kissed his forehead.

She would figure this out. There was always the chance the new owner would let her rent from him, though she doubted it. She knew Mr. Potter had given her a below market deal on the rent because he'd been a close friend of her father's.

Bella wanted to figure this all out before people started asking her questions. She didn't want to start accepting help now. Not after she'd come so far on her own.

She closed the door slightly to the boys' room and went back to her computer. The hours slipped away as she searched for rental spots for her store and a place for her and the boys to live.

She closed the lid on the laptop in the early hours of the morning and headed for bed. She had found nothing. Nothing at all that she could afford.

* * * * *

Owen got back to Comfort Crossing early evening the next day. He had made a quick run into New Orleans to look at a property in the warehouse business district near the French Quarter. His research team had sent him a preliminary report on a restaurant there and he wanted to take a look at it in person. Putting a restaurant in a larger city, known for their fabulous food, would be a new business opportunity for his company and he had been debating heading in that direction. As long as he was learning the restaurant business anyway, he might as well branch out. He had liked the area and the research said that part of the city was booming with fancy restaurants and hotels converted from old warehouses. He had sent a report back to his team of further information he needed before he could come to any decision.

He had driven back to Comfort Crossing in the dwindling light. His stomach growled, reminding him he had once again skipped lunch. He pulled into a parking spot outside Magnolia Cafe. Might as well sample something else from their menu. Besides, the restaurant was comfortable, welcoming, and he wanted to try another piece of their delicious pie.

He got Becky Lee as a waitress again and a table by the

window. Just a few minutes later, Izzy came into the cafe. He waved at her as soon as she spotted him. She gave him a friendly wave back, then paused to speak with Becky Lee.

Izzy was dressed in a print skirt, practical flats, and a simple green knit top. He bet the green of the blouse brought out the emerald in her eyes. If she would just come a little closer, he could tell.

The next thing he knew, it was like Izzy had read his thoughts. She threaded her way through the tables toward his.

"Hi, Owen." She flashed him a smile and he could see that, yes indeed, the blouse did bring out the emerald shade in her eyes.

He pulled away from staring at her eyes. "Hi there. You eating alone?"

"Just going to grab a quick dinner."

"Do you want to join me? I haven't ordered yet." He thought it would just be a welcome change from eating alone, that was all.

She paused for a brief moment, then nodded. "That sounds nice. Becky Lee always feels like she has to hover over me if I'm in here eating alone." Izzy slipped into the seat across from him.

"You need to see my menu?" Owen held it out to her.

Izzy laughed a friendly laugh that poured over him in melodious waves. "No, I pretty much have it memorized. Been the exact same thing for years. Keely, the owner, keeps trying to change it, but her mother shoots her down every time. I guess her mother is technically the owner, but Keely has run the cafe ever since her father died quite a few years back."

Owen was amused at the fact that Izzy knew the little details in the cafe owner's life. He doubted if anyone around his condo in Chicago off Michigan Avenue knew a thing about him, much less anyone in the building where his company was located. He had a fascination with small towns, which probably led to him investing in businesses in small towns and helping them turn a profit. Okay, it might have been because his father had always run the company by buying out businesses and closing them. When Owen took over the company, he started doing the exact opposite of his father, he helped to make them profitable.

Becky Lee came over to their table. "So, you two are going to eat together? Good. Hate to see people eating alone. Izzy, glad you decided to come in and eat instead of skipping yet another meal. You work too much, you know that? You should eat more regular meals. What will you have? We're out of the beef stew."

Owen listened while Becky Lee rushed through her spiel, a little lost in her staccato jumping of topics. Izzy didn't even blink at the chastisement or the ramble.

"I'll have a burger and a vanilla shake." Izzy turned and looked at Owen.

"I'll have the same. Fries come with that?"

"Sure do." Becky Lee nodded as she jotted down their order. She turned and headed back towards the kitchen.

"I'd really like a cold beer with my burger, but Keely's mom won't let her get a liquor license for the cafe." Izzy nodded toward the front of the cafe. "That's Keely up there in front with the long brown hair."

"So Keely runs the cafe, but her mother makes the decisions?"

Izzy grinned at him. "That about sums it up."

He was glad he got to make his own decisions about his company without answering to anyone else. He was pretty sure that he was past the point where he could ever deal with having a boss or having his decisions second guessed. He hadn't had to deal with that since his father had passed away.

Owen watched as Izzy's long slender fingers unwrapped the napkin roll of silverware and carefully placed the implements on the table. Her nails were painted a pale pink color, perfectly manicured, no chips on the polish. He noticed she fidgeted a bit with the silverware.

"So, your boys. How old are they?" He figured people always liked to talk about their kids, right? That's what he'd heard anyway.

"Jeremy is ten, Timmy is seven."

"They're cute boys." They were, with their curly brown hair. Too bad they didn't get their mother's shiny red hair, though maybe a boy wouldn't like the red hair as much as a woman. Who knew? He knew little to nothing about boys. Or kids in general.

"They are cute, but they're a handful. Sometimes I want to throw up my hands and say that they win." She grinned at him. "But, of course, I'm just nuts about them. I can't imagine my life without them. They bring me so much joy."

Owen thought that parents were a strange breed of humans. He couldn't understand their private society, didn't know the secret handshake. But he could see how much the boys meant to Izzy by the sound of her voice and the light in her eyes when she talked about them.

"You have any kids?" Izzy's question caught him off guard.

"No, no kids." He doubted he ever would either. He never really found much time for dating women. The few he had dated got tired of the limited time he had with them, or his constant trips away. To be honest, none of them had really captured his attention. He sounded shallow, even to his own ears.

Though, in some strange way, Izzy had caught his eye in just a few short days. It was new to him to not only be attracted physically to Izzy, and he couldn't deny he was, but he wanted to know all about her, too.

Becky Lee brought over their dinner and they carried on a comfortable conversation over their meal. Izzy was easy to talk to, and quick to laugh. Her smiles popped up on her face and made her eyes sparkle with warmth.

"So, how long have you known Becky Lee?" Owen asked yet another question. He couldn't seem to know enough about the woman sitting across from him.

"Oh, most of my life. She's great. I don't know what I'd do without her. And Jenny. That's our other friend. The three of us, well let's just say they keep me sane."

They finished up their meal, but Owen was loathe to see Izzy go. Becky Lee brought the checks to the table way too quickly for his liking. He reached out and took both checks. "This is on me."

"Oh, you don't have to do that."

"No, I want to. It was nice to not eat alone for a change."

"Do you eat alone a lot?"

"Most of the time." Either out grabbing a quick bite to eat, or alone at his condo. Yes, most of his meals were alone.

"Mine are mostly filled with constant chatter and spilled milk." Izzy grinned at him again.

He had no idea what it would be like to have family with you for most of your meals. He hadn't even had that growing up. His parents had sent him to boarding school. When he had been home, his parents went out to eat often, leaving him at home with a nanny, a tutor, or the housekeeper, depending on his age. His parents had traveled often, too. On their rare visits home they would question him about grades, goals scored, and honors achieved.

Izzy's boys must have quite a different childhood than he'd had. A mother who cared and actually sat down to eat with them. Who took them to the park to play soccer with their friends.

"Well, thank you for dinner then." Izzy's words poked through his thoughts.

"You're welcome." What else could he say to keep her here?

Izzy stood up. He reluctantly pushed away from the table and stood up, too. He went up and paid their bills, with a generous tip to Becky Lee. After all, she was the one who'd introduced Izzy to him.

"Bye, Bec. See you soon." Izzy waved to Becky Lee.

Owen held the door open for Izzy, and she slipped deliciously close to him and out the door into the cool night air. They stood in the lamplight, Izzy so close to him that he could smell the faint scent of ginger or orange or something near that. He heard her sigh. It sounded like a contented sigh. A good meal and nice night kind of sigh. He hoped.

"I should go." Izzy turned to him.

"Yes, I should too." But he didn't want to. "May I drive you home?"

"No, I'm just a quick walk away. Thanks, though."

She turned and left him, the light from the street light casting highlights in her red hair as she walked down the sidewalk.

He climbed into his car, and headed to the Sweet Tea.

Chapter Five

Bella sat with her laptop, again searching for rental property. She'd been surprised to find that there were no suitable places to rent. When had the Main Street area gotten so popular? She knew the town was having a much needed revival, but she'd been unable to find a place to rent, much less in her price range.

Discouragement flooded through her. She'd been trying for days to find another option for the shop. Rental prices on Main Street for the few spots she had found were out of her budget.

She'd gone and seen one place that she'd hoped would work for the shop, but the space had been in such need of repair and the owner hadn't been willing to help clean up the space. She needed, okay wanted, a spot with character like the building she was in now. Her displays helped sell her items. She tried to let her customers envision what the items would look like in their own homes. A beat up, tired store room didn't seem like it would work for her business. But all that didn't matter, because the rent was twice what she paid now.

Bella looked up from her laptop to see Jenny enter the shop. Her friend came over to the counter and plopped a package on the counter. "Old books I found in the attic. Thought you might like to use them in one of your displays. Oh, and an old milk glass vase."

Bella reached into the bag and pulled out the vase. She had just the spot for it. "Thanks."

Jenny and Becky Lee quite often found little items for her to add to her displays and she appreciated their help.

Jenny set her purse on the counter. "I heard a rumor that Mr. Potter sold the building. Is it true?"

Bella knew her friends would find out eventually. She'd hoped to have an alternative plan in place before she told them. She didn't want them to look at her as a failure.

"It's true. Well, Mr. Potter said he'd tell me when it was finalized and ask the new owner if he'd rent to me. Since I'm on a month-to-month lease, I don't have time to mess around. I need to find another option for the shop in case the new owner won't rent to me. Oh, and a place to live." Bella tried to keep the despair out of her voice. This wasn't Jenny's mess to fix.

"You should have told Bec and me. Let us help you."

That was the whole problem. She didn't want someone helping her. She wanted to do this on her own.

56

"I thought I'd have it figured out before you heard about it."

"I wish you'd let me help. I have some savings you could borrow for deposits."

"Thanks, but I'll figure this out."

"You don't have to do everything on your own."

"I don't want you to be out money because I failed." Failed. That's what it felt like to Bella. A failure. She could just imagine Rick's I-told-you-so litany that she was sure to hear before long.

"That's silly. You didn't fail. You've got a successful business. We're just going to have to find you a place to reestablish it."

"Honestly, I haven't found even one place. Not even on the side streets. I thought maybe I could find something on Rosewood Avenue. That area is getting built up, but nothing for rent there that I could find."

"Maybe the new owner will let you stay on." Jenny, always the hopeful one.

"Maybe, that's the hope I'm hanging onto right now. But I need to be prepared."

"Let me know if you change your mind and will let me help you."

"I'm not going to change my mind, but I really appreciate the offer."

"Well, I have to go run pick up Nathan." Jenny gathered up her purse. "He's so grounded right now— he's got detention. Again."

"I'm sorry, Jenny. I'm sure he'll work it all out soon. He must miss Joseph so much."

"I know he does, but he's going to have to find a new way of working out his emotions. Cutting school isn't a way to fix things. I've taken him to a counselor in New Orleans, but nothing seems to help." Jenny sighed.

"Jenny, you're a good mother. Things will work out. I know they will. Nathan's a good kid."

"He is. I have to keep reminding myself of that fact." Jenny stepped away from the counter.

"Thanks for the books and the vase."

"You're welcome. I'll see you tonight for dinner."

Jenny left the shop and Bella turned back to the laptop. A rising panic ran through her. What if all her hard work the last few years amounted to nothing in the end?

She flipped the laptop closed, unwilling to believe she'd looked at every commercial rental property in the downtown area of Comfort Crossing. She picked up the milk glass vase that Jenny had brought and headed over to an old table under a window in a back room. A lace tablecloth covered part of the table, but left part of the beautiful wood of the table showing. The table was set with four table settings of some old china. Hand-embroidered napkins were rolled and placed on each plate. She carefully set the vase on the middle of the table. She'd put some fresh flowers in it tomorrow.

This she knew how to do. To set up displays. To find furniture and antique items to sell in her shop. To display beautiful vintage clothing. The thought of starting over and all that entailed poured over her like a pounding rain during a summer storm. She couldn't bear to lose her shop. It was an intricate part of her now.

She slipped into a chair at the table and looked across at the many displays she'd fashioned in this room. She sat there, alone, facing failure and an uncertain future. Again.

Bella adjusted a plate on the table, making it just right. She shook her head at the whole pity party thing. She would figure this out. She would.

* * * * *

That evening, Jenny stood in the doorway to her house and didn't even let Bella get inside before she started questioning her. "Okay, what gives? Becky Lee called this afternoon and told me you had dinner with some guy named Owen last night."

Bella gave her friend a quick hug, not surprised that Jenny already knew about her dinner with Owen. Becky Lee was nothing but thorough in keeping them all informed of what was going on with each other.

"I just happened to run into him. He's here on some kind of business. He was eating alone, I was eating alone…"

"How did you meet him?"

"I met him the other night at Magnolia Cafe, then ran into him at the park the other day with the boys."

"Becky Lee says he's right good looking. I need to stalk

him and see what he's like. See if I approve of him." Jenny grinned.

"Yes, I guess he is good looking." Who was she trying to kid? The man was drop-dead yummy handsome.

"Well, it's nice to see you going out."

"I didn't really go out, Jenns. I just ran into him at the cafe."

"Close enough. Becky Lee said he paid the tab." Jenny turned and walked toward the kitchen. "I'm going to grab a bottle of wine and we'll sit on the porch until dinner is ready. Nathan is over at his grandparents', so it's just us. Nathan and I needed a break from each other."

Bella did like Nathan. He was a good kid. But he'd been getting into a handful of messes since Jenny's husband, Joseph, had died. She figured Jenny could use a non-stress night. Plus, Martha and William, Joseph's parents, were good people. They were very involved in their grandson's life, and attended all his sports games and school events. Yes, a night apart was probably what both mother and son needed.

Jenny came back with a bottle of white wine and two glasses. They went outside and sat on two rockers on the front porch. It was a perfect temperature for sitting outside. A warm breeze drifted lazily through the magnolia trees lining Jenny's long driveway. The heady scent of the flowers in the beds along the porch teased through the breeze.

Jenny let out a long sigh.

"Tough week?" Bella asked her friend.

"I'm ready for school to end. I love teaching, but I love my summers off, too. You know, unless Nathan manages to flunk one of his classes. Then I'll be hauling him to summer school, because I'll take away his driving privileges. I swear, the boy is brilliant, but he's just barely picked up a book since Joseph died. I know he's upset and misses Joseph terribly, but he needs to find a way to put his life back in order before he screws up chances for college. I think he's coming around a bit. Maybe. I actually saw him bring home his calculus book."

"He'll be okay soon. He just needed some time. Maybe the summer off will be good for him. Is he going to work part time for his grandfather again?"

"Yes, thank goodness William lets Nathan work at his law firm. I secretly think he's grooming Nathan to want to go to law school and take over the firm. But, Nathan would have to pass his classes to do that," Jenny said wryly.

"It's only been this last semester or so that his grades have fallen, hasn't it? I'm sure his teachers understand."

"Maybe understand too much. I think they cut him some slack and he just pushes for more and more excused assignments. It's got to stop."

"You have any plans for the summer?"

"I was thinking of taking Nathan for a week's vacation to the beach. If we go to the island do you think you and boys could get away? That would be so much fun to vacation together."

"A lot depends on what happens with my lease and my store. And if we need to find a new place to live."

"You guys could always move in here while you look for a new place. It's certainly big enough."

"Oh, I don't want to inflict my boys and their noise on you. You forget how loud young boys are. Constant motion."

"It wouldn't be inflicting. I love your boys."

"Well, I hope to just find a new place right away if we have to move. Though, since my lease is month-to-month, a new landlord has really no obligation to me at all. It's such a mess."

"If you need anything—cash for a bit— whatever, you'll ask me, won't you?"

"I appreciate the offers, but I've done all this on my own, and want to keep doing it that way." Bella took a sip of her wine. She was so proud of all she'd accomplished with the store and supporting the boys after the divorce. She didn't want to take help now. She relished the independence and financial freedom she'd scraped together for them. Even if it wasn't a lot of money she made, it was enough to keep them comfortable.

"It's okay to accept help, you know. My help wouldn't come with demands, or even suggestions on how you do things."

Bella sighed. "I know, I just want to do this by myself."

"Okay, but the offer stands. Moving in here for a bit or

some help with finances if you need it."

Bella knew that Jenny, and Becky Lee for that matter, would do anything to help her. She just hoped she could figure it all out for herself because there was no way she would let herself become part of her friends' responsibilities.

"So, back to this Owen guy." Jenny changed the subject.

"What about him?"

"You going to go out with him again?"

"I didn't go out with him…"

"Maybe you should ask him out."

"Jenny, I barely have time to breathe these days, much less date someone. Between the boys and the store, I'm plumb exhausted."

"I could help out at the store this summer. It would be fun. I love your store. You have such a great eye on finding just the right items to sell and putting it all together."

"Jenny, really, I appreciate all your offers, but your life is busy enough without adding in my problems."

"I wouldn't mind."

"I'll figure it out, Jenns. Don't worry about me." Bella just hoped she was right, that she could pay the new amount of lease payment if the new owner even wanted to rent to her. Or if she could afford a new place for the store and an apartment for the boys. She ran her hand through her hair. She hated that everything was so up in the air right now.

Well, soon enough she'd find out her fate with the store and apartment. Maybe she should just be glad for the time she had until it all fell apart. Or maybe the new owner would lease it for the same amount and let them still live above the store. She'd hold onto that hope for as long as possible.

* * * * *

Jenny cleaned up the dinner dishes after Izzy went home. She wished her stubborn friend would take some of the help she'd offered. Jenny wasn't surprised, though. Izzy just wanted to make it on her own after Rick left. She admired the determination, but hoped that a new landlord wouldn't blow up Izzy's carefully constructed post-divorce life.

Her phone rang and she smiled, sure it was Becky Lee wanting to catch up on any news.

"Hey, Jenns." Becky Lee's voice came over the phone.

"Hi, Becky Lee. What's up?"

"How was dinner with Izzy? Did she talk about Owen?"

"She insists it was a chance meeting, which I guess it was, but it was nice that she finally had at least dinner with another male. I know she hasn't been on one date since Rick left."

"I've tried to set her up. Lots of times. She just turns me down. I know she's busy, but every woman deserves a bit of fun in her life. And my offer is there for you, too. I could fix you up."

"I'm not ready to date. Not ready at all. It's just too soon." Jenny balanced the phone between her ear and her shoulder and continued to clean up the kitchen.

"Well, the offer stands."

"You'll just have to keep trying with Izzy. Sooner or later she has to date someone again."

"Yes, it's probably not smart to push her to go out with some guy who is just in town for a bit. But I thought it might be good, I don't know, training for real dating."

Jenny laughed. "A training date. That's an idea."

"Did Izzy hear anything on her lease yet?"

"No, not yet. I wish she'd let me help her, but she is so stubborn. She wants to do it all by herself. The girl does love her independence."

"Well, I don't blame her for that. She's come a long way in the last few years. Made everything happen herself. Made her own choices. After Rick commanding what she wore, what she cooked, what she drove, I don't blame her for wanting to do things on her own." Becky Lee's voice reflected the pride she felt for her friend.

"She did, and I'm so proud of her. Her parents were so controlling, too, and she just always was the wanting-to-please daughter." Jenny wiped off the counter and hung up a dish towel while they continued their conversation.

"Like when she wanted to go away to Tulane for college, but they insisted on the community college. Or do you remember when she wanted to be a cheerleader in high school and her father insisted only fast girls were cheerleaders. So she dropped out of tryouts."

"I do. She always let other people make her decisions. It drove me nuts. I love the new, improved Izzy and her independence. This shop, and making her own decisions has been so good for her. But, this whole losing the lease is just an unlucky break." Jenny sighed.

"Maybe the new owner will still let her stay there and won't up the rent." Becky Lee didn't sound very hopeful. "Well, I'll let you go. Just wanted to check in."

"Okay, night Bec."

Jenny hung up the phone. Her dog, Choo Choo, looked up from where he was curled up in the corner. "You want to go out one more time?" The black lab mix stood up and stretched and walked over to the door. Jenny opened the door for him.

She mindlessly continued cleaning her kitchen. Guilt washed over when she realized she was glad to have Nathan gone for the night. She was tired of their endless arguments. Tired of the constant struggle. She'd tried everything possible to get him back on track with his life. She missed the fun-loving son he had been before Joseph's illness and death. She sometimes felt like she'd lost both Joseph and Nathan, and couldn't get used to how lonely she felt at times.

As much as she looked forward to the summer, she was afraid it was going to be a long one. She no longer had Joseph to sit outside with in the evenings and talk about their days. Nathan barely said two words to her at a time and she couldn't remember the last time he'd hugged her. He used to be so affectionate, but now he was all walled up in his own little world.

Oh, Joseph.

What she wouldn't give to be able to talk through things with her husband now. She had so many regrets about their relationship, things she wished she'd done differently. Maybe the harsh reality and loneliness of being a widow was her penance for all the mistakes she'd made and secrets she'd kept.

Her heart was heavy in her chest and she fought to blink back the tears that threatened to fall. She missed the life the three of them had once had. The family they'd been.

Choo Choo came back and barked once at the door, pulling her from her melancholy thoughts. Jenny let him back in. "All set for the night, Choo?" She reached down and petted the dog. He wagged his tail and started to walk off towards the stairs. She could swear sometimes that the dog understood everything she said. She gave one last look around the kitchen, flicked off the lights, and headed upstairs, grateful for Choo Choo's companionship.

Chapter Six

Owen wanted to close the deal with Mr. Potter to buy his building. It looked like all the paperwork would be finished within the week. Then he'd talk to Jake. Or Jake's mother. They wouldn't say no if it was a done deal. Probably. His brother sure was stubborn. Hopefully it would all fall into place. The lease for the shop in Potter's building was a month-to-month lease, so that wouldn't be a problem. Mr. Potter had said he'd notified the tenant that the building was up for sale. They were probably looking for a new space already.

It was all working out. The building had an apartment upstairs, and he figured that Jake and his mom would move back in there. That's where they'd lived for years before they sold the building. His offer to Mr. Potter was a fair one, and he was glad when the man agreed to take it. No unpleasant surprises with this deal. It looked to be wrapping up fine, just like he liked.

He looked outside his window at the Sweet Tea. The sun was shining and calling him to come outside. He really had nothing to do on this deal until tomorrow, so he decided to walk down Main Street and go have lunch at another restaurant he'd seen called Best Friends Diner. He wanted to look over that restaurant, too. He needed to check out all the restaurants in the area. Research, of course. Magnolia Cafe had good food, really good, but it was simple, plain food. He already had the wheels turning on looking into getting a liquor license. He thought a nice wine list along with beer and mixed drinks would add a different offering from the usual diner fare when Jake and his mom reopened their restaurant. If they opened it. If they'd accept his offer.

He went downstairs and saw Rebecca cleaning the front room. She looked up and smiled when she saw him. "Going out for a bit?"

"I thought I'd walk down to Best Friends Diner for lunch."

"It sure is a nice day for a walk. I've opened the windows down here to air everything out. Just a lovely day. Larry's out puttering in the garage under the guise of fixing a lamp for me. I reckon he just wanted to get out before I put him to work with the spring cleaning."

"I don't have much time for walks back home, so I figured I'd take advantage of the time and the weather while I'm here." The only walking he did back in Chicago was on a treadmill at the gym in his condo building.

Well, and back and forth to his office, which was barely a block from his condo.

He headed out into the spring sunshine and strode down the street. He realized he was walking at his normal brisk clip, but there was no need to hurry. He slowed down to a leisurely stroll, the gait felt unnatural to him.

His thoughts went back to the notes he'd taken about the town. He hoped that Rebecca would be glad to know he was helping to open another restaurant in town. He figured it would help draw more people into town, which could only help all the businesses, like Rebecca's bed and breakfast. Last weekend the town had been filled with shoppers. The antique shops looked like they'd done a bustling business as well as the other gift shops around town. He'd noticed a women's dress shop that had a steady stream of customers too. The art galleries had been full of not only people looking, but he'd seen a handful of customers come out with wrapped pictures in their possession. The town was a perfect mix of quaint, crafty, antiquing, and charm. He hoped the town would welcome him, an outsider in their midst. Heck, he hoped Jake would start to consider him more than an interloper. So far everyone—but Jake that is—had been welcoming, and he enjoyed that.

It didn't take him long to reach Best Friends Diner. He crossed inside and noticed they were doing a brisk business at the end of the lunch time rush. He waited a moment for his eyes to fully adjust from the bright sunlight to the lights in the diner. He looked around the restaurant and noticed Izzy sitting at a table near the back. She was going to think he was stalking her.

Izzy sat with papers spread out in front of her, a look of concentration on her face. She lightly drummed her fingers on the table as she studied the papers. He wasn't sure if he should interrupt her or not. *Oh, who was he kidding, of course he was going to go say hi.*

He walked back to her table. "Hello."

Izzy looked up at him with her pretty green eyes. "Ah, so we meet again."

"It appears we eat on the same schedule."

"And there are only two places in town to eat on Main Street. Do you want to join me?"

Owen looked at the files spread out on the table in front of her. "I don't want to disturb your work."

"No problem. Just crunching some numbers. I could use the break." She stacked her files up and pushed them aside.

"I just ordered. I'll get Kat back here to take your order."

"Is she one of the best friends part of Best Friends Diner?"

Izzy's infectious laughter spilled between them. "Yes, one of three."

He ordered his lunch and settled back in the booth. "So you have the day off?"

"The afternoon. Have to take Timmy to a doctor's appointment this afternoon at Doc Baker's. Just a checkup. Then the boys have baseball practice."

"They keep you pretty busy."

"Pretty busy in an understatement. We seem to always be at some sports practice or game. Or school thing. Or fighting over homework. But I wouldn't change a thing. Well, maybe have them not wear through the knees of every pair of pants in like three weeks flat." She smiled.

He couldn't imagine that. He hadn't had the type of childhood where you could just wear your jeans and go out and play. It was organized sports with uniforms. Uniforms at the schools he went to. He couldn't remember a time when he'd ever worn out the knees of a pair of pants.

"So they play a lot of sports?"

"Baseball, basketball, soccer."

"That's a lot."

"But they love it and it wears them out. A tired boy is a… well, a tired boy. A good thing."

"I suppose it is."

Kat brought their food and Izzy regaled him with stories of the boys. Her face was animated when she talked of her sons. Her graceful fingers kept tucking her hair behind her ears until she finally twisted her hair up at her neck and stuck what looked to be some kind of stick, similar to a chopstick, through the twist of hair. He was amazed it stayed in place. Mostly. Just a few tendrils of her red hair framed her face. He liked the look. Liked it a lot.

* * * * *

Bella looked across the table at Owen. He had an irresistible smile and his eyes lit up when he laughed. She hoped she wasn't boring him with tales of the boys. She'd rambled on and on, she knew that. Okay, she admitted that Owen made her a bit nervous. She wiped her hands on her napkin and tucked a fly away piece of hair behind her ear. Again.

It was too bad Owen was just here for a few days on business. She had to admit, he was the first man she had even been remotely interested in since Rick left. Not that she'd ever admit that to Becky Lee and Jenny, they'd hound her to death. Owen was dressed more causally today in a knit shirt and slacks. She wondered if he even owned a pair of jeans. No, he was here on business, that's probably why he was always dressed so nicely. She still wasn't sure she could picture him in jeans. Or shorts. He just seemed like a dress nicely kind of man.

She glanced down at her years-old skirt and shoes that had seen better days. She just didn't have the money now to buy things for herself, so she made do with what she had. She'd tied a bright scarf around her neck today, though, to brighten up the otherwise muted outfit. She was pretty sure the only semi-new things in her wardrobe were hand-me-downs from Jenny. And she was pretty sure that Jenny had only worn the items a time or two—if that— before giving them to her, saying she just didn't like the way they fit. Jenny always made sure the things she gave to her friend were bright and cheerful.

To be honest, she didn't mind not having much to spend on herself. The days of shopping for clothes that Rick approved of were long behind her. She shuddered when she thought of the closet full of dull, stuffy, prim and proper clothes she'd bought when they were married. They were the only kind of clothes that garnered Rick's begrudging approval. She'd given away almost every item of clothing to A Second Chance charity when Rick moved out. She'd only kept a few basics and the few things that had some color to them.

She was okay with things the way they were. She was proud of her store and making it on her own. After the divorce, Gil had given her half the value of their parents' house. It hadn't been much, the house wasn't worth much money. But he'd insisted, since he'd moved into their house after their parents had died. She'd used the meager money, plus a small loan from Gil, to do minimal renovations and buy merchandise.

But all of this success from her hard work might change at any minute. The uncertainty was eating at her.

"So, do your boys go to their father's often?" Owen's question interrupted her thoughts.

"Every other weekend. Plus a few other days here and there. They'll be with him Wednesday. We share or split holidays. Or we sometimes juggle the schedule based upon our workloads." Mainly juggle based on Rick's schedule, but she made it work for her.

"So you and your ex get along okay?"

Bella sighed. "Mostly. It was rough at first, but we basically get along okay now." Because she was the peacemaker and rarely argued with Rick about the boys' schedule. He changed the schedule to meet his whims, and she just went along with it and fit her schedule to his. It was just easier that way. He'd even decided—for her— that she wasn't going to work while the boys were little. Well, at least until TheNewMrsHardy caught Rick's eye. Then he'd been perfectly fine with Bella going to work and making her own way. Only he'd hated that she'd started her own business and told her repeatedly that she'd never make a go of it.

"I imagine it makes it easier on both you and the boys if you get along."

"Well, it was a bit rocky at first, when Rick said he was leaving. I was so shocked. I had no idea he was even unhappy. But we got it sorted out." Izzy was glad that the shock of separation and the legal hassles of the divorce were behind her now. She had a civil relationship with Rick, usually, as long as she let him have his say. In a weird way she was glad how things had worked out. She would have never opened her shop when they were married since Rick wanted her at home all the time. She realized now that it had always been his wishes and desires that were fulfilled in their marriage, though even that hadn't kept him happy.

Oh, but how she liked making her own decisions now, no one telling her what to do. She was actually very happy with her life. Except for the whole lease thing.

She looked over at Owen, enjoying his cup of coffee. His strong hands wrapped around the mug instead of using the handle. He had on an expensive watch. No other jewelry. His brown hair was cut precisely in a businesslike haircut. It suited him.

He looked up and smiled at her just then. Her heart did a little dance which surprised her senseless. She sure hadn't felt that in a long time. She smiled back at him. Yes, it was a darn shame that he was only in town for a bit. She was frankly all out attracted to the man. Dashing and charming, in a bit of a formal businesslike way. What was not to like?

She forced herself to quit her fantasy of actually going out on a date with the man. She reached for her purse to pay her bill, not wanting him to pay for her meal again.

"So would you like to go out Wednesday night while your boys are at their father's?"

That caught her off guard. Did she? Well, she did, but she didn't. There was so little time in her life to date. But the only plans she had for Wednesday night were a hot bath and a book. A date with Owen sounded better. Much better. *Answer the man.*

"Yes, I'd like that."

"What would you like to do? Dinner? Movie?"

"There's a park outside of town a few miles. Really pretty. Live Oak Park. It's such nice weather. I could pack us a picnic."

"That actually sounds like a great idea."

"I have to take the boys out to Rick's house, which is in the direction of the park. How about I pick you up at five, we'll drop the boys off, and head out to the park?"

"I could pick you up."

"No, I'll do it. I have the boys' sports equipment in my car, they have ball practice that Rick will be bringing them to."

"Okay, five it is."

Kat came over with their bills and Owen reached for them.

"No, I've got mine, but thanks."

He just nodded at her and pulled out some bills from his wallet to pay his tab. She did the same and slipped her money into the leather folder with the check.

Owen flashed his smile at her, and her heart did that two-step dance again. Wednesday night should be interesting. She couldn't decide if she was bursting to tell Jenny and Becky Lee about her date, or if she wanted to keep it to herself for a bit. Of course her friends would kill her if someone saw her out on a date and told either Jenny or Becky Lee before Bella had a chance to tell them.

Yes, she'd call them both up and tell them. A date. She

was going on a date.

Then it hit her. Well, darn it all. She'd offered to make the picnic. Big mistake. He was going to find out just what a lousy cook she was.

* * * * *

Owen was pleased with the deal he'd made with Mr. Potter. Mr. Potter was going to notify his tenant that she had until the end of the month to move out. He'd be ready to convert the building at the beginning of the next month. Just a few small changes. It really was a fabulous building just as is.

Then, of course, he had to get Jake and his mother on board. That was next on his to-do list. He was heading out to meet them and hoped they'd agree to his plan.

Extending his stay didn't bother him a bit. He was actually pleased to have a reason to be in town for a while longer. He had the picnic with Izzy tomorrow, and hoped to see more of her while he was in town.

Izzy had totally captivated him. Her quick smile. The sound of her laugh. Her thick red hair and how it caught the sunlight. The word besotted came to mind. An old fashioned word, but it seemed to fit him right now. He shook his head at himself.

He hadn't had a date for just fun in, well, he couldn't remember when the last time was. He usually just asked out women for different functions in Chicago. Charity events. Business affairs he needed to attend.

But just for fun? To spend time with a woman? He

couldn't remember the last time. He was always too busy with his work. He had no desire to marry into a business relationship like his parents had, either. There had been little love lost between his parents, mostly just a partnership to help his father on his way up the corporate ladder. He'd needed the pretty wife on his arm. His mother played the part, and his father had showered her with trips and presents. They'd both been happy in their own sort of way, he guessed. Not that he really knew, because if truth be told, he really hadn't known his parents very well.

Owen put aside his thoughts of his parents and continued walking down Main Street and past the park, hoping he'd run into Izzy, but no luck. He caught a reflection of the silly grin he had on his face in a storefront window, the silly grin put there from looking forward to the picnic tomorrow. Izzy would probably be surprised that he'd never gone on a picnic in his life. Ever. He knew it involved picnic baskets and blankets. He figured he'd pick up a good bottle of wine to bring.

He whistled a bit of an off-key rendition of some silly love song as he walked down the street to the Sweet Tea. Whistling. Owen Campbell was whistling. Probably for the first time in his life.

Yep, besotted. Fit him perfectly. *What kind of a man called himself besotted?* He was so in over his head.

* * * * *

Jake watched as his brother—half-brother—walked up

the cobblestone path to his aunt's house. He and his mama had been staying with his mama's sister for the last six month or so. Before that they'd stayed at his uncle's house. He'd say one thing about their family, they were always there for each other. One side of his family, anyway.

But, he needed to find them a place to stay of their own soon. He'd needed the help taking care of his mother while she recovered from her cancer surgery and treatments. She seemed to finally be getting back to normal. Whatever normal would be like after living through what she had in the last few years.

Besides working in a restaurant in the French Quarter in New Orleans, Jake had taken every odd job he could find the last few years to bring in extra money after he'd been forced to sell their building on Main Street. The profit from the sale of the building had mostly gone to pay off medical bills. His mom now worked part time at her sister's flower shop. He felt like it was time to move on. He'd saved up a tiny bit of money, and hoped to be able to find them a small place of their own. He still didn't want his mother living alone.

The knock on the front door brought him back out of his thoughts. His brother was tenacious, he'd give him that.

"I'll get the door." His mother got up off the sofa, crossed over to the front door, and opened it. Sunshine spilled into the front hallway. "Hello, Mr. Campbell."

"Please. Call me Owen."

"Okay, Owen. Come inside."

Jake watched his brother walk into the front room. He didn't know why Owen stuck around. Jake had made it pretty clear that he didn't need a brother barging into his life.

"Jake, good to see you again." Owen held out his hand.

Jake reluctantly took his brother's hand. His brother had a firm handshake. A businesslike handshake on smooth hands that had probably never seen five minutes of any kind of manual labor.

Jake's mother motioned for both of the men to sit down. Jake sat on the sofa next to his mother. Owen took the overstuffed chair across from them.

"Let me get right to the point." Owen leaned forward in his chair. "Jake has made it clear that he wants nothing from our father. I understand that. My—*our*—father was heartless in denying Jake's existence. But, the fact remains, we are brothers whether Father acknowledged him or not."

Jake started to interrupt Owen right there, but his brother held up a hand to stop him.

"Please, let me finish."

Jake gritted his teeth but did as Owen asked.

"I've bought back your building on Main Street. I've set up an escrow account for taxes on it for the next ten years. You can open up your restaurant again and live upstairs if you'd like."

"We don't need charity. I already told you no." Jake tried to control his temper. His brother was a hard-headed fool and was just not getting the picture.

"It's not charity. You are as much Father's son as I am. I'm sorry he wouldn't acknowledge you, but it doesn't change the facts. You are just as entitled to his inheritance as I am."

"Don't want it."

"Jake." His mother's voice was soft but strong.

He turned to face her.

"I think we should listen to Owen's offer. His father knew you were his son. He did. When I found out I was pregnant, I told him about you. He offered me money to just... go away. I turned him down and never contacted him again. But it doesn't mean that you're not his son, and aren't due something from the man. You are his flesh and blood."

"I don't need his money."

"Jake, sometimes you can be so stubborn. I know you're angry that he never got to know you. Pretended you didn't exist. But you are letting your pride get in the way of a good opportunity."

"But—"

His mother reached a hand over and touched his leg. "I would love to have the building back. It means so much to me. It's been in my family for generations. I love every single thing about it. The floors, the windows, the location on Main Street. My family history is so entwined in that building. I'm strong enough to run the restaurant again. This is something I would love to do."

Jake looked at his mama, then over at Owen, who'd been smart enough to keep quiet while his mama talked.

His mother touched his face and smiled at him. "You are a proud man. I understand that. But just because Stephen Campbell chose to not claim you as his son doesn't make it so. I was angry with the man for years and years. But cancer gives you a new perspective on life. I'm no longer angry, but Stephen did owe you, Jake. He should have taken responsibility for his actions. Owen wants to make up for that. Let's take Owen up on his offer. Open up the restaurant again. I loved it so."

Jake could never refuse his mother anything. "If it's what you really want, I'll help you open it again. I still say the man owes me nothing."

"How about you look at it as something your brother wants to do for you? Your brother who does acknowledge you." Owen said.

Jake didn't want a single thing from his brother—not for himself—, but he could see the light shining in his mother's eyes, her excitement about getting her beloved restaurant back.

"Fine. Agreed."

"Ms. Landry, I was wondering if you would mind talking to me a bit about the restaurant."

"Sylvia. Please call me Sylvia."

"Sylvia, I've been looking at the restaurants in town

and the growth in the area. I was wondering if you'd consider opening up a different kind of restaurant than you had before."

"Her restaurant did fine how it was." Jake was tired of his brother, tired of his know-it-all attitude.

"Let's hear what Owen has to say." His mother looked expectantly at Owen.

"There are already a handful of good home-cooked meal type restaurants in town. The only fancier place is out at The Plantation Inn outside of town. It's only open for dinner on the weekends. I wondered if you'd consider opening up a restaurant that had a different kind of menu. We could get a liquor license for wine, beer, and drinks."

Jake watched in amazement as his mother nodded in agreement.

"I think that's a fabulous idea. I always cooked the same thing and had the same menu as my mother had. She only had it a few years before I took over. But I love to try out new recipes. I bet we could come up with a menu of items that would be different, but reasonably priced."

Jake had to admit that his mother loved to experiment in the kitchen. She'd gone through a French stage of cooking and an Italian stage. He couldn't even remember all the different types of cooking she'd experimented on for them. But she had always just done plain, homestyle cooking at the restaurant.

"The other idea I had was to open the second floor as a tea room type area. You would also rent the area out for events. Possibly use that first floor smaller room for a coffee shop area for some good coffee and pastries for the morning crowd."

"Look, Owen. You're moving too fast. Are you saying that if we take this building, we have all these strings attached?"

"Not at all. I'm just used to researching businesses my company buys. It's what I do, see how companies can help their bottom line."

"I think you have some very good ideas, Owen. I'd like to see the research and hear more of your thoughts." His mother said.

"Great. I'll get you a copy of my research and we can meet in a few days to discuss."

"I'd like that." His mother broke into a big smile. "Oh, and we'll have our own place to live again. My family will be as excited about that as I am."

Jake was unsure about this whole deal, but could see how happy his mother was. He'd do anything to make her happy after the hard couple of years she'd had. "We're going to have to hire lots of help, Mama. You can't overdo it."

"If you like to experiment with recipes, maybe you could come up with a menu and we'll get a cook in. I know you did a lot of the cooking before, and of course you can again, but I thought a chef from New Orleans that I have my eye on might like to move here for the job. You'd, of course, do any interviewing of staff. I've put aside projected expenses for the first year in an account for you."

His mother's eyes sparkled with excitement. "I'm going to go find my recipes right now and start working on what we could have for a menu."

"I'll get that research over to you and we'll meet again soon." Owen stood up.

"One thing, Owen. I don't want you telling people about... us." Jake stopped his brother.

"You mean that we're brothers?"

"Exactly. It's no one's business. I don't want the town talking about my mother again."

"You have my word." Owen nodded.

His mother got up and crossed over to Owen. Her slender arms wrapped around the surprised Owen and she hugged him.

"Thank you, Owen. You are a very kind man."

"You are very welcome, Sylvia. I feel like it's too little, too late. But I'm very glad you accepted my offer."

Jake stood by the window and watched his brother walk back down the cobblestone pathway. So much had changed in the last hour. He wasn't sure he liked it. He still didn't want anything from a father who refused to admit he existed. But he couldn't deny his mother was happier than he'd seen her in years. And Stephen Campbell owed her at least that, even from the grave.

Chapter Seven

Jenny and Becky Lee sat on the queen bed in Bella's room as she stood in front of the full length mirror holding up two sundresses.

"The light teal one." Jenny's voice was decisive.

"No, the floral one." Becky Lee was just as sure of herself.

"Thanks a bunch, guys. You're so helpful." Bella looked at both dresses, holding up one and then the other in front of her. "I give up."

"Okay, go with the floral one that Becky Lee likes. I like it too."

Bella couldn't remember having this hard of a time picking out an outfit to wear since her high school days.

"Maybe I should just call him up and cancel the date."

"Or maybe you should just get dressed and quit worrying about everything. You'll have a fabulous time." Jenny got up from the bed and walked over to Bella. "Put on this floral dress and those cute sandals. I'll pick out a necklace."

"I haven't been on a date in so long I won't even know how to act. What in the world will we talk about? Thank goodness you made most of the food for the picnic, Becky Lee."

"Some nice sandwiches, an appetizer that isn't messy to eat, cheese and crackers and peach pie. It was no problem. We all know how much you love to cook." Becky Lee laughed and joined Jenny at the dresser and dug through Bella's jewelry. "I like this twisted bead necklace. That will go great with your dress. Wear these cute earrings with it, too."

"You're a life saver, Bec. My cooking, other than mac and cheese, spaghetti, or peanut butter and jelly is nonexistent these days."

"Izzy, your cooking skills have always been nonexistent," Becky Lee teased.

"Don't brag. We know you're the best cook and baker in the county." Jenny turned to Becky Lee. "Did you bring me a piece of your pie?"

"But of course. It's in Izzy's kitchen."

"You're the best," Jenny said.

Bella slipped on the bright floral sundress. She'd bought it the day after Rick had said he was leaving, a minor revolt against his dictates of always dressing in muted tones. She ran her hand down the smooth cotton. She hadn't had much money to spend on herself, but this dress always made her feel independent. It was a silly thing for a dress to do, but it did. Becky Lee came up behind her, dropped the necklace around her neck, and fastened the clasp. Bella turned and looked in the mirror again. Yes, she still loved this dress.

"Wear your hair down." Jenny declared.

"You guys aren't giving me much choice this afternoon."

"Because you aren't making any decisions." Becky Lee rolled her eyes.

Bella had to agree with that. She couldn't make up her mind about what to make for the picnic or what to wear. Fortunately, or unfortunately, depending on how she looked at it, her friends had descended upon her with helpful advice, decisions, and most of the food for the picnic. Of course she'd expected no less when she had told them that she had a date tonight.

"Mom? You about ready to go?" Jeremy's voice came through the door.

"Just a minute. Almost ready."

She took one last glance in the mirror. "We better go."

The three friends walked out of the bedroom and into the kitchen.

"Wow, you look nice, Momma." Timmy glanced up with a hint of surprise in his eyes.

Bella wasn't sure that was a compliment or not. Did she usually not look nice? She smiled at her son, deciding to take it as a compliment. "Thanks, sweetie."

She picked up the picnic basket and they all filed down the backstairs and out into the late afternoon sunshine. The boys piled into the car and Bella turned to her friends.

Jenny gave Bella a quick hug. "Have fun."

"Gotta get to work." Becky Lee waved as she headed for her car. "Call me tonight when you get home. I want to hear everything. Y'all have a good time."

Bella got into her car. She babied that car, hoping to get many more years use out of it. Gil had fixed the broken window, thank goodness. She couldn't imagine having to take on a car payment now, much less buy a car outright. "Seat belts fastened?"

"Yep." Her boys answered in chorus. They knew her car didn't start until their seat belts were on. She hoped it carried over into their teen years when they became drivers and she wasn't there to remind them. Better to make the habit while they were young.

She pulled out of her parking space behind the building. Jenny waved to them as they pulled away.

"We're going to stop and pick up Mr. Campbell on our way to your dad's house." Bella glanced in the rear view mirror at the boys.

"That guy from the park? How come?" Timmy questioned her.

"Mr. Campbell and I are going to Live Oak Park."

"Are you going on a date?" Jeremy entered the discussion.

"Well, I guess you would call it a date. We're going to have a picnic dinner."

"Why do you want to date someone?"

Bella could see Jeremy's scowl when she glanced in the rearview mirror again. "I just enjoy spending time with him."

Bella pulled up to the Sweet Tea. Owen was waiting outside. He walked up to the car, opened the passenger door, and climbed inside. He was holding a small canvas bag.

"Hi, Izzy. Hello, boys."

"Hi, Mr. Campbell. You're going on a date." Timmy announced.

"I guess I am."

Jeremy sat in stony silence. She knew he wasn't pleased, but she couldn't have him acting rudely.

"Jeremy, aren't you going to say hi to Mr. Campbell?"

"Sure. Hi." There was no warmth or enthusiasm in his voice.

"You have to fasten your seat belt, or the car won't go." Timmy explained helpfully.

Owen looked a bit confused. "Sure thing."

"You should always wear a seat belt." Timmy explained like he was talking to a small child.

"That's a very good rule." Owen answered.

Owen pointed to the bag he had with him. "Wine, compliments of me, and wine glasses compliments of Rebecca. Oh, and wine opener."

"That sounds nice."

They pulled away from the Sweet Tea and headed toward Rick's house outside of town. Timmy chattered the whole way about school, baseball practice, and what a great cook his stepmother was. *Lovely.*

Rick came out of the house as she pulled up in front of his home. From the few times she'd been inside, she knew that TheNewMrsHardy had decorated it with style. The woman could cook, decorate a house, and the boys said she even helped them with their homework. She guessed it could be worse, they could have an evil step-monster stepmom.

The boys opened their doors and ran to their father. "Dad, Momma has a date. They're going on a picnic." Timmy tugged at Rick's hand and pulled him down closer. "Miss Becky made the pie and stuff for picnic but told me not to tell. You know, 'cause Momma doesn't really cook." Timmy's exaggerated whisper floated back towards them.

It just kept getting better and better. She looked over at Owen who seemed to be a bit overwhelmed with the bedlam that surrounded her boys. Maybe. She couldn't really read him.

Rick came up to the passenger side of the car and Owen rolled down his window. Her ex stuck his hand out. "Rick Hardy."

"Owen Campbell." Owen took Rick's offered hand.

She could see Rick size up Owen in the obvious way

he always did. He sized people up the moment he met them and filed them into the category he thought they fit, a habit of his that had always annoyed her. He made snap decisions on whether he would bother with a person or not. She could see him take in Owen's expensive slacks—for a picnic—nice shoes, pricey watch.

Then Rick turned to her with a look that said "How did you snag this guy?"

Bella deliberately ignored the look. She wasn't going to let Rick get to her.

"I'll see you tomorrow at the ballpark." Rick stated it more than asked her.

"Yes, I'll be there. I know they both have games at the same time."

"Boys, get your stuff out of the car. Pop the trunk for them."

Bella was sure Rick meant to add a please to his command. She popped open the trunk and the boys grabbed their sports equipment.

"Bye, Mom." The boys waved as they raced into the house.

Rick nodded at her and stepped back from the car. She put the car into gear and drove down the long driveway to the main road. Maybe dropping the boys off on the way to their picnic hadn't been one of her best ideas.

* * * * *

Owen wasn't sure what to make of the last fifteen minutes of his life. He was certain that Jeremy didn't like him,

Timmy probably did, Rick didn't for sure.

"I'm sorry." Izzy glanced at him as they pulled away from Rick's house.

"Sorry for what?"

"For the kid ambush. For Rick…"

"Not a problem."

"Well, hopefully the rest of the evening will go more smoothly, you know, now that the secret is out that I can't cook and Becky Lee provided most of the picnic."

"That's not a problem. I can't cook either. We'd starve to death, I guess, if it were up to us."

She smiled at him then, and seemed to begin to unwind. Good. He hoped they could have a nice, relaxing time. A picnic. Before he could think of how strange it sounded he blurted out, "This is my first picnic. Ever."

"You're kidding me, right?" Izzy looked at him with wide eyes.

"Honest truth." His admission shocked him probably as much as it surprised Izzy. He never blurted out anything. He always carefully thought through his words before speaking, a trait that served him well in the business world.

"Wow, the pressure is on then. I hope it lives up to what you think a picnic should be." She drummed her fingers on the steering wheel as she waited at a stop sign.

"Since I have no preconceived idea, I'm sure it will be great."

"Surely you have some notion of what to expect. You've seen picnics on TV and movies."

"But those are fiction, this is real."

"Just so you realize there are flies at real picnics and sometimes ants."

"Okay, I'll be prepared for anything."

He watched her as she drove, trying not to be obvious. She had on a casual floral sundress and sandals, her hair was down and drifted around her shoulders in waves of golden red. The breeze coming through her half-opened window made her hair float around her face. She kept tucking it back behind her ear.

He was probably overdressed, but he hadn't really brought any clothes with him that were appropriate for a picnic. Nor shoes. He glanced down as his leather loafers. She probably thought him a fussy dresser. He should really pick up a pair of jeans or maybe even shorts and some casual shoes if he stayed here much longer.

There he was, already planning on spending more time with her. He wondered what it was like to grow up in a town and still live there as an adult, for people to know you when you passed them on the street, what it felt like to really belong to a town. To fit in to a place. To have life-long friends. He could only faintly imagine these things. Izzy was a lucky woman.

He looked back over at Izzy. Her lean legs stretched out beneath the dress. Her legs had a bit of tan already though, somehow, he didn't think Izzy had sat out tanning. It was probably from watching the boys' ballgames and taking them to the park.

He noticed she drummed her fingers against the steering wheel almost every time she made a stop. Her painted nails made a subtle click sound. He was fascinated watching her painted nails tap the wheel.

Owen wasn't sure when he had taken in so many details on a woman. It was like his business mind, the one he usually tapped into for discovering every little detail about a business he was interested in, had flipped and started recording every little detail about Izzy. She intrigued him.

* * * * *

Bella wondered how much longer Owen would be in town. It seemed silly to date a man who lived halfway across the country, and yet, she was glad she'd said yes to his invitation. He was a bit overdressed for a picnic, but she guessed that he hadn't brought any more casual clothes—not knowing he'd be going on his first picnic. First. The concept of never having gone on a picnic boggled her mind. He wasn't just from a different city, he was from a whole different world.

But, he intrigued her. The first man she had been interested in dating since, well too many years to count. Her last date with anyone, before marrying Rick, had been in high school. So, yes, it had been a long time.

"Here we are." She pulled into the parking lot.

"It's beautiful." Owen's voice held an edge of awe.

"It is pretty isn't it? I love the way the live oaks frame that pathway. There are a couple gazebos with tables, or we can just put the blanket down where ever we want."

"The blanket sounds fine."

They got out of the car and Owen took the picnic basket and his bag with the wine and glasses. She grabbed the blanket and headed over to her favorite more secluded spot near the edge of the park. A family was having a barbecue at one of the gazebos. A father pitched a ball to his young son. A few couples wandered along the paths. A lazy evening of fun at the park.

Bella led Owen down the main pathway through the live oaks, and turned onto a smaller path. She felt his hand brush against hers, then again. He finally took her hand in his. His hand was strong, but not rough. Warm. When was the last time anyone had held her hand except for her boys? It felt nice to just walk along in companionable quiet. She led him down the trail until they came out into an opening with a large tree and a couple of big boulders.

"We'll set up here." She pointed to the large tree.

Owen set down the picnic basket and helped her spread out the blanket. It was an old blanket that she'd had since high school days, a bit tattered since it had seen its share of picnics and ball games. She sank down onto the blanket and kicked off her sandals.

"This is nice." Owen looked around the clearing.

"Jenny, Becky Lee, and I used to come here. Still do

sometimes. It's peaceful."

Owen sat down beside her on the blanket. Close, but not touching. "Would you like some wine?"

"Yes. That sounds nice."

Owen deftly opened the wine. She was impressed. She always had to wrestle a bit to get wine open. His fingers grazed hers as he handed her a glass. She had an overwhelming urge to tangle her fingers up with his and connect, but she just took the glass and sipped her wine.

Owen sat near, looking at her, not quite staring, not quite not staring. She felt a flush of warmth rise through her.

"The sun just lights up your hair."

She self-consciously flipped her hair behind her shoulder. "My hair is always going every which way. Has a mind of its own."

He leaned closer and moved a lock of her hair away from her face, his hand trailing gently across her check. "I like your hair."

Her breath caught and her heart tripped. His soft touch seared her, branded her with longing she hadn't felt in years, waking a part of her that she had hidden in the daily bustle that was her life.

She wanted to reach out and touch his face. Watch his eyes. See his reaction. But, of course, she didn't. She didn't quite have the nerve.

She cleared her throat. "I should get dinner set out." She busied herself with pulling out all the wonderful food Becky Lee had made for them. At the last minute, Bella had packed real plates and silverware and cloth napkins. Owen just had seemed like the real plate kind of guy. Especially since she now knew he'd never been on a picnic.

They filled their plates with food. Owen looked so relaxed, but she felt like she was strung tighter than the line she had stretched across a wall of her shop to hang some prints. She obviously didn't have the same effect on him that he had on her. She watched him pick up his wine glass and she followed the glass right up to his lips. Strong lips. Not quick to smile, but when they did it transformed his face from stuffy businessman to charming, approachable man.

She turned away, trying to get the image of his lips out of her mind. She grabbed up her sandwich and took a bite. Only to choke. Tears came to her eyes, and Owen moved closer and patted her back.

"Are you okay?"

She nodded, still coughing a bit. Gah, she was making such a horrible impression. He knew she didn't cook, and now it appeared she couldn't eat. "Just went down the wrong way." She finally managed a few words.

Owen stayed right by her side. His arm brushed hers, lighting a fire between them that she was afraid burned only in one direction.

She took another sip of wine, waiting for her breathing to settle. But it was impossible to breath with his arm against hers, his warmth sinking into her skin.

Owen reached his hand up and pushed yet another unruly lock of hair away from her face. This time though, he didn't take his hand way. It hovered near her face, until he reached his knuckle under her chin and tilted her face up to his.

Maybe the burn did go both ways.

His lips lowered to hers, gentle, questioning, then more insistent. She leaned up into the kiss, feeling her heart tapping wildly and her breath coming out in little wisps of air.

He pulled back away a bit and she felt like she was free falling. She wanted to crawl right back smack in the middle of that kiss. He looked at her and the heat of his gaze burned her face, filling her with a passionate ache deep inside.

"I've wanted to do that since the first time I saw you." Owen's voice was low.

"Really?"

"Ah, yes. Really. I'm inexplicably drawn to you even though I tell myself we just met." He traced a finger across her lips.

His finger, so gentle on her lips, lit a fire within her. She could easily be talked into abandoning all reason at this point. She wanted this man.

"Let's try one more kiss." Owen leaned forward.

Yes, sir. Let's. Her mind spun out of control.

Owen kissed her again, a long and lingering kiss. A kiss

that was more shared with her, than claimed her. A kiss that made her lose all rational thought.

Owen took her into his arms, pulling her close. She could feel his heart beat against her. He wasn't as calm as she'd thought. Owen leaned back, lying down on the blanket, and pulled her with him, kissing her the whole time. His warm hands roamed over her arms, her back.

She finally pulled away, just a bit, to look at his face. She could see the desire in his eyes now. How had she ever thought he was hard to read?

Here she was, in the county park, necking with Owen like they were teenagers. She kissed him again, her breath coming out in disjointed huffs. *Hmm, maybe acting like a teenager wasn't all bad.*

Owen finally pulled his lips away. His wonderful, warm, kissable lips. He sat back up, leaned against the tree, and settled her by his side. He draped his arm around her shoulder.

She waited for her breathing to get back to normal and her thoughts to settle out of their whirlwind of emotions. So many thoughts. How good it felt to lean against him. How she could feel his heartbeat where she had her arm placed across his chest. What a great kisser he was.

Then her thoughts spun to the fact she barely knew the man, he lived states away, and what the heck was she doing? She struggled to turn those thoughts off and get back to thinking about his kiss.

"I could kiss you for hours, but I guess that won't get

our picnic finished, will it?" His voice was low, sexy, and rumbled across his chest where she rested her head.

"Finished picnics are over-rated."

Owen laughed. "I wouldn't know. But here, let's eat. Your friend went to all the trouble to make our dinner."

Bella reluctantly pulled away and sat up. She sat crossed legged with her legs tucked under her skirt. "I'll try to eat without choking this time."

"That would be nice." He smiled at her.

"You want some of the pie? Becky Lee makes the best pie."

Owen nodded, and she cut him a piece of pie then handed it to him, sorry their hands didn't touch. He took a bite. She was entranced by the fork, watching it scoop up a bite of pie and move up to his lips.

There she was. Back to his lips again. She deliberately looked away, taking in the view of the clearing, watching some birds dart around from branch to branch.

"Izzy?"

"Yes?" She turned back to look at him.

"Think I can kiss you again when we finish the picnic?"

"I think that'd be okay." A smile teased the corners of her mouth.

"So that's the official way to end a picnic?"

"I think we could definitely make it a new rule of picnics."

Owen set his empty plate down and leaned towards her. "Just one more kiss."

With that, she was lost in his kisses once again. Far away from her life and responsibilities. Just enjoying Owen, enjoying herself and happy in the moment.

* * * * *

Bella was still reeling from Owen's goodnight kiss. He'd given her a take-your-breath-away kiss before starting to get out of her car when they got back the Sweet Tea. He'd opened the passenger door, then leaned over one more time with another long kiss that had made her feel drunk with desire. She could still feel the fire of his kisses as she walked up the stairs to her apartment.

She laughed when she walked in the door to her apartment. The phone was ringing, and she was sure it was Becky Lee.

"Hi Bec."

"How'd you know it was me?" Becky Lee's laugh came across the phone lines.

"I knew you couldn't wait to hear the details. I bet you've been calling every fifteen minutes."

"Every five. So, how was it?"

"It was nice." Bella dropped her purse on the table, and slipped off her sandals.

"Nice? That's what I'm going to get? Nice?"

"Really nice."

"Come on, Izz. I reckon you can give a girl a bit more to work on."

"He's a good kisser."

"Ah, that's my girl. So, he kissed you." Becky Lee

paused. "So, was it weird to kiss someone besides Rick after all these years? You okay?"

"I thought it would be strange, but it wasn't, not really. I guess it's been a bazillion years since I've kissed someone besides Rick. Well, there you have it. A milestone. Now I don't have to worry that I've forgotten how to kiss."

If she had forgotten, Owen had sure shown her how it was done. Over and over again.

"So, how much longer is he going to be around town?"

"I don't know. The only thing I know, from talk around town, is he's somehow connected to the Landrys. Maybe a friend of theirs? He was there at their BBQ last week. We didn't really talk about it. We haven't really talked about our jobs or anything. I'm not even sure what he does for a living. See, I'm so out of the dating game, I don't even know what I'm supposed to talk about. Besides, it was nice to *not* talk about the shop or my lease problems, just to forget about them for a night."

"You should search him out on the internet. See what you can find out."

Bella stifled a yawn. "Maybe I will. Tomorrow, though. I'm fixin' to get up early. I have a new display I want to set up at the shop."

"Okay. Sleep well, Izz."

"Night, Becky Lee."

Bella turned out the lights and crossed into her bedroom in the darkness. She flopped down on her bed, fully clothed, and stared into the darkness. She wasn't certain what she was getting herself into with Owen, but one thing was for sure... she wanted to see where things were headed. She wanted to go out with him again. And she sure as all get out wanted him to kiss her again.

Chapter Eight

Owen sat at the breakfast table at the Sweet Tea. Rebecca had made a delicious breakfast and he was relaxing with a second cup of coffee.

"Mind if I join you?" Rebecca came in with a mug of coffee in her hand. "I'm letting the skillet soak. Thought I'd take a little rest."

"No, please, join me."

Rebecca sat down across from him. "So, are you here for much longer?"

"Yes, actually, I need to be here for a while longer. Do you still have room for me for a bit?"

"Yes, that's not a problem. We have a group coming this weekend, but I'll still have room for you. Larry will be pleased that we'll be completely full."

"Great." Owen wasn't in the mood to change to another place to stay. He liked Rebecca and Larry's B&B. He liked being able to walk to everything here in town.

Then, of course, there was Izzy. He sure wasn't ready to say goodbye to her yet.

"Have you been finding things to keep you busy? I know a small town must be very different than Chicago." Rebecca took a sip of her coffee.

"I have. Been taking my time exploring the town. Even went out for a picnic last night."

"Really? Who with?"

"Izzy Hardy."

"Who?" Rebecca wrinkled her brow. "Izzy Hardy? Oh, you mean Bella Amaud. Everyone calls her Bella, except Jenny and Becky Lee, who for some reason have always called her Izzy. Both nicknames are short for her real name, Isabella. She owns Bella's Vintage Shop down the street. She goes by her maiden name again since she and Rick split up."

The world tilted and spun around him.

No, he couldn't possibly mean Bella Amaud. He meant Izzy Hardy. Not the woman who owned Bella's Vintage Shop. The shop in the building he had just bought for his brother. The woman who was getting kicked out of the building at the end of the month.

Izzy. Isabella. Bella. His heart plunged.

"She owns Bella's Vintage Shop?"

"She does. She's done a fabulous job with it. Built it all up on her own after her husband left her. She lives above it with her boys. Didn't she tell you?"

The sinking feeling got worse. He was going to throw

Izzy and her boys out of their home too? Things couldn't get more messed up. He sure hadn't put the name Bella with Izzy. She was going to hate him, and he didn't blame her one bit.

"You okay? You don't look so good." Rebecca peered at him closely.

"Well, it appears I've made a bit of a mess of things."

"What do you mean?"

"I've bought the building that she has her shop in. I gave it back to my brother and his mother. It had been in their family for generations."

Rebecca put down her mug. "Your brother? Jake Landry?"

Owen was so rattled that now he had broken his promise to Jake. He'd told about their connection. "Well, darn it. I didn't mean to say that. Yes, Jake is my half-brother. I just found out a while ago and came to find him. My father never acknowledged him, but that doesn't make it right. He *is* my brother. This seemed like the least I could do for Jake and Sylvia. But, please, I told Jake I wouldn't talk about our relationship. It's Jake's decision to tell people about us if he wants. It appears he doesn't want to."

Owen now could add breaking his promise to Jake to his list of transgressions in this town.

"I won't tell anyone. We'll let Jake figure it out in his own time. I'm sure Sylvia will love having her building back. Is she going to open the restaurant back up?"

"Yes, but a different kind. A fancier one, serving wine and beer. She's actually all excited about figuring out a new menu. They're planning on living upstairs in the apartment."

A brief worried look crossed Rebecca's face. "Well, I know the town could use a nice restaurant with all the business we're getting here these days. I reckon Sylvia is so excited to have a restaurant again. But poor Bella. It was such a nice arrangement for her."

Owen scrubbed his hand over his face. "Not that Magnolia Cafe or Best Friends Diner aren't nice. They are. Comfortable. Good food. This will just offer up a different kind of food. Nice wines."

Rebecca looked worried. "I hope Bella can find a new place for her shop and a new place to live."

"I didn't know that Izzy owned that shop, or that she lived above it. I just didn't connect the dots. Now, it's too late. I've given it to Sylvia and Jake. Sylvia is so happy. I heard that she's just recently recovered from cancer treatments. I thought it would give her a reason to, well, jump back into life now that she's feeling better." Owen leaned back in his chair. "I've really done it this time."

"You just need to explain it to Bella. I'm sure she'll understand. I'm just worried she'll have a hard time finding new space."

"Maybe she'll let me help her."

"Don't count on it. She's become very independent and self-sufficient. She'll probably want to figure things out for herself. It's just a bad break for her." Rebecca looked out the window. "I like that the town is having a rebirth of sorts. Lots of artsy businesses. Couple of clothing stores. We're getting a lot of people moving here that commute into the New Orleans area for work. We could use a nice restaurant, too. It only helps all of us for the town to attract new business. But I still feel for Bella." Rebecca sighed. "But, I admit, I'm very, very happy for Sylvia. She deserves something nice in her life now. Never knew anything about Jake's father. Figured it was none of my business. There were rumors at the time he was born, but the town soon moved on to new gossip, as small towns do."

"Yes, he's my brother. He doesn't seem too keen on having a brother though."

"Just give him time. It must hurt to be totally rejected by your father."

"I'm sure it does. But I'm not sure he didn't get the better deal. Being raised in that family. A big normal family."

"The Landrys are one big family, that's for sure. Fine people. Every one of them."

Owen sighed. "But I can't believe it's Bella's shop in the building I bought. Mr. Potter said the tenant's lease was month-to-month and he told her he was selling the building, but I didn't know it was her." He hadn't really thought about the person behind the lease and how it would affect her. He had just wanted to get the building back to Jake and his mother. He hadn't really looked into the renter since the lease was month-to-month, he knew he wasn't going to renew the lease.

He was mad. Mad at himself. He usually did a much better job of finding out every little thing about the properties he bought. Mr. Potter hadn't mentioned that Izzy lived above the shop with her boys either.

Everything was just one fine mess and he had muddled it all.

* * * * *

Jenny sat at a table at Magnolia Cafe. The breakfast rush was winding down, and Becky Lee should have time to chat pretty soon. Which was good, because boy, did she need to talk to her. Then they needed to go see Izzy.

Becky Lee slid into the seat across from her. "Okay, what gives? You said you had something to tell me?"

"First, did you talk to Izzy last night? Did she have a good time with Owen, or was it a one-time deal?"

"Oh, she had a good time, all right. They kissed. I gather he's quite the good kisser."

"I was afraid of that."

"Afraid he was a good kisser?"

"No, afraid that she had a good time and she was getting emotionally tied up with him."

"You don't like him? Becky Lee looked confused.

"Well, I searched for him on the internet. Just wanted to check him out for Izzy. We've got a problem."

"What, he's married? Wanted for murder?" Becky Lee

leaned forward.

"Worse."

"Spill it, Jenns."

"He's a developer. He buys up businesses and properties. He bought Izzy's building."

Becky Lee sat for a moment "He's the one going to buy out Mr. Potter?"

"I checked with Mr. Potter. Izzy's building has already been sold. And Owen told Mr. Potter to tell Izzy she'll have to move out." Jenny hurt for her friend. Izzy was going to be crushed. Not only was she losing the shop and her apartment, she was losing it to the first man she'd been attracted to in forever.

"This isn't good. Do you think he was trying to trick Izzy?"

"I don't know. But I'm sure Izzy doesn't know this about him. She would have said something, and I seriously doubt she would have dated someone who was going to throw her out on the street."

"Bless Izzy's heart. What a mess. I reckon we've got to tell Izzy though." Becky Lee straightened her shoulders. A smiled teased the edges of Jenny's mouth. Becky Lee was getting ready to go to battle for their friend. They could always count on Becky Lee.

"I thought we could walk over to her shop when you're finished with your shift?"

"Ah, you don't want to tell her alone, do you?"

Jenny sighed. "The whole don't-shoot-the-messenger

came to mind. Besides, she'll need moral support. Do you think he was ever going to tell her? Was he just playing with her, keeping her busy until the deal went through?"

"I don't know, but I have a few choice words for the man." Becky Lee pushed up from the table. "Give me a few minutes, I'll get things wrapped up and be ready to go."

Jenny sipped on her coffee and looked out the window at Main Street. She could see two other storefronts where new stores were going in. Izzy would have a hard time finding a new location on Main Street, much less one with the rent as reasonable as what she paid now. Then, there was the whole living situation.

Izzy had worked so hard to make her shop a success and be able to financially take care of her boys. Rick had been vocal about how Izzy would never make a go of the shop. Izzy had proven him wrong.

Oh, Rick was going to have some choice words to say to Izzy when he heard about this. The man was always putting in his two cents... well, really his couple of dollars, on and on... where it wasn't wanted or needed. What a self-centered jerk. She never had figured out what Izzy had seen in Rick.

Jenny felt helpless, and didn't like that feeling one bit. It didn't seem fair that some outsider could swoop into town and take it all away from her friend. Owen Campbell was a devious man, keeping all this a secret from Izzy.

* * * * *

Bella looked up to see her friends come walking in the door to her shop. She waved to them and gave them a just-a-minute sign while she finished checking out her customer. The customer had bought a big armoire that had been refinished with off-white chalk paint and delicate flowers painted on its door. It was a good sale for her, especially if she had to pay to move her store somewhere else. It wouldn't hurt to have the heavy pieces of furniture already sold.

Jenny and Izzy walked up the counter as her customer left.

"Hey. What's up?"

"We have news," Jenny said.

"What kind of news?"

"The kind you don't want to hear." Becky Lee chimed in.

Bella pulse quickened. She didn't need bad news. "Okay, just tell me."

"Your building has been sold." Jenny looked at her. "I found out who bought it."

"Who? Maybe I can talk him into letting me stay and not raising the rent too much."

"That's a no go, Izz. Hasn't Mr. Potter called you today?" Becky Lee reached out and touched Bella's hand.

"He left a message that he was stopping by this afternoon. Why? I'm losing the lease, right?" Bella

115

sighed. All dreams of having an easy solution to her shop and her living quarters rushed out the door into the warm spring day. The sun shone outside, mocking her with the optimism she had secretly held that things would work out.

"Afraid so. And there's more," Jenny said.

"What could be worse than that? I don't get the weeks left until the end of the month to find a new place and move out?"

Becky Lee cleared her throat and glanced over at Jenny. "It's who bought the building... it's Owen. I heard he already has a new renter."

Bella blinked her eyes. Her heart pounded in her chest. *Owen? Her Owen?* And why the heck had she thought of him as her Owen? "What? Owen bought the building? Why would he buy it?" She realized she'd never really asked him what his business was in town. Her error. He probably had known she owned the shop the whole time and was just... what... toying with her? A small town fling to pass the time while he was here?

She pasted a smile on her face, knowing it was probably not fooling her friends. "I sure know how to pick 'em, don't I? First date since Rick and I divorced, and I go out with the guy who hides the fact he bought out the building my store and home are in and he's renting it to someone else. What do you think that's all about?" She sank down on the stool behind the counter, her mind reeling with random thoughts. She needed to find a place to live, immediately. If she couldn't find a new place for the store by the end of the month, maybe she could move the store's merchandise to the back room at her brother's Feed and Seed until she could find a new location.

"I'm not sure why Owen didn't tell you." Jenny moved behind the counter and put her arm around Bella. "Let us help you, please. You could move in with Nathan and me for a bit. Give you more time. We'll help you look for new space for your store."

Bella couldn't help the sinking feeling of failure. She had worked so hard to get herself set up and on her own two feet. She couldn't bear to be back borrowing money, living with someone else, uprooting the boys. She could hear Rick's voice, playing over and over in her head. *I told you so.*

"Jenny, really, I appreciate the offer, but I can't descend on you with the boys. But I will take any help or leads you guys have about finding another storefront. Even two months ago, there were openings on Main Street. I don't think there are any right now."

"We'll ask around. We'll find you something that works. I know we will." Becky Lee sounded positive, but then she was always a half-full kind of person.

Bella needed to borrow some of that positive outlook.

"Well, I hope so." She had to find something else she could afford. She wasn't going to let all her hard work on getting Bella's Vintage Shop up and running be for nothing. Besides, she loved her shop, loved finding just the right items to sell, loved setting up her displays, loved chatting with her customers. The shop was intertwined with who she was now.

The bell over the door interrupted her thoughts. All three women looked up when the door to the shop swung open.

Chapter Nine

Owen walked through the door of Bella's Vintage Shop and saw Izzy, Becky Lee, and another woman. There was not a friendly look in the bunch. He squared his shoulders and started across the distance of the shop, filled with more unease than he ever had when facing a hostile board of directors.

"Izzy, can we talk?"

"I'm not sure there's anything to say."

Well, that answered that question. She knew that he bought the building. He sucked in a deep breath. He had to explain and make her understand.

"I didn't know that Bella's Vintage Shop was yours. I didn't put it together. I didn't put the Izzy Hardy I knew, with Bella Amaud who was on the lease." He desperately wanted her to believe him. His heart beat with a glimmer of hope that she would believe him and they could… what? Did he actually think she would ever date him again? He'd be lucky if she didn't take the antique cane that was sitting on the counter and whomp him upside the head.

Becky Lee turned to the other woman. "This is the man who is throwing Izzy out on the street. Jenny Bouchard, meet Owen Campbell."

Jenny flashed a look of outrage at him and turned to look protectively at Izzy. "Well, I can't say it's a pleasure to meet you, Mr. Campbell."

Izzy looked up hopefully. "Can I lease my shop back from you? And the apartment?"

"I can't lease it to you, Izzy. I'm sorry. I have… other plans."

Izzy studied him slowly with a look of hurt and anger. "I find it strange that you come to town, turn up where I am, then ask me out on a date. Then you say you just found out that I own the shop."

"I didn't know."

"But you were okay with throwing this unknown Bella out on the street?"

"I didn't know. I needed *this* building. Mr. Potter said the renter was month-to-month."

"I see. It doesn't matter who you step on to get what you want." Her voice was cool with an edge of barely suppressed contempt.

"It's not like that. I offered Mr. Potter a good deal on the building and he seemed pleased to be able to move out of town to his brother's."

"I'm supposed to find new space in just a few weeks?"

"Mr. Potter said he told you when I first offered to buy the building. I assumed you were already looking for new space."

"A lot of assumptions going on there, bud." Becky Lee chimed in. "I think it might be best if you just leave. You've done enough."

"I'd like to talk to Izzy, if that's okay."

"I have nothing to say to you, Mr. Campbell. I'll be out by the end of the month." Izzy face was frozen into a hard, unfeeling stare.

He felt his heart tug with an unfamiliar pang. He wanted to protect her. But from what? From him?

"Why don't you give her more time to find space for the store and a place to live?" Becky Lee walked right up to him, her finger pointing dangerously a fraction of an inch from his chest.

"I... can't" He felt like he was everything the women thought he was, and worse. But he had promised the building to Jake and his mother. Sylvia was already full of plans. He had a renovations crew scheduled for the beginning of next month.

"Izzy, I didn't know you and the boys lived upstairs either. I'm so sorry." He hated the hurt look in her eyes, the look she was trying so hard to hide from him. "Let me help you find a new space. Help you find a place to live."

"I don't need your help. You've done enough."

Jenny pinned him with a no nonsense look. "I think it's

time for you to leave." She had an arm protectively wrapped around Izzy's shoulder.

Owen looked questioningly at Izzy. She nodded her head. "Yes, you should go."

He gave Izzy one more look and slowly turned away, his steps echoing on the wooden floor. The very unfamiliar feeling of defeat washed over him. He walked out the door, leaving behind the shambles he had created of Izzy's life by trying to help out the brother he had never known he had.

* * * * *

Bella slumped against Jenny after Owen left. Her friend held her tighter.

"It's going to be okay," Jenny murmured.

Bella fought back the tears that wanted to fall. She wouldn't let them. She was going to get through this. It was just a setback. A major one. But she wasn't going to let Owen Campbell get the best of her. Her mind kicked into planning mode. She wasn't going to wallow in despair.

"I need to go talk to Gil. See if I can temporarily put the merchandise from my store in the back room at the Feed and Seed. I'm sure he has room."

"We'll help you move. Becky Lee can round up some of the guys from Magnolia Cafe. Nathan will help."

"It's just that I won't be making any income until I can find another place for the shop."

"I wish you'd let me loan you some money," Jenny

offered again.

"Jenns, I love you, but no, I'm not taking your money. I'll work it all out." But how was she going to work it out? She had hardly any money in savings. Was it just a week ago that she had been so proud of herself that she had actually begun saving a bit after only two years in business? It had been a short-lived heady feeling. She had been so proud that she was finally making a success of her life. All on her own.

A group of women came into the shop. Bella pasted on a smile. "Welcome. Let me know if I can help you with anything."

She turned to her friends. "I've got to get back to work."

"Are you going to be okay?" Becky Lee's eyes held a worried look.

"I'll be fine. I'll go talk to Gil after work and see if I can store my things there until I find a new place to lease."

"I'll ask around and see if anyone knows of a place for you and the boys to live. Nothing better than a job at Magnolia Cafe to keep my finger on the pulse of the town. We'll find you something." Becky Lee turned to Jenny. "We should go let this woman get back to work."

"We've got your back, Izz." Jenny hugged her.

"I know. Love you guys."

She watched as her friends left the store. Just like Owen had. Owen, the first man she'd been interested in years. The man she had kissed. Kissed lots. And enjoyed it thoroughly.

No more of that. She felt so betrayed by him. The weight of all the decisions she had to make, and all the work she had ahead of her slammed against her, making her feel alone and frightened for the first time in a very long time. She resented Owen for making her feel that way, too.

She wondered what her brother, Gil, was going to say about all this. He'd always been overprotective. He might put a bounty on Owen's head, or at the very least, chase him out of town. Which was what she wanted, wasn't it? For Owen to be gone?

* * * * *

Bella pushed into the Feed and Seed that evening, figuring her brother would still be here. He worked even longer hours than she did. She needed to talk to Gil, then get over to the ballpark to see the boys' games.

"Hey, Bella. What brings you here?" Gil walked out from behind the counter. He was a handful of years older than she and had looked out for her since their parents had died. Actually he had looked out for her ever since she was a toddler following around in his shadow. He was the one who had first called her Bella and the nickname had stuck.

"I need to ask a favor."

"Yes." Her brother grinned at her.

"You don't even know what I'm going to ask."

"Have I ever said no to you?"

"Well, yes you did. In high school I wanted you to set me up with your friend, Tex."

"The guy was a loser. He wasn't really my friend and there was no way in Hades that I'd have let him go out with you."

"Okay, probably a good choice, but I was so mad at you then. Anyway, it proves that you have said no to me."

"Ancient history, Sis." He led her over to an old wooden table. "Pop?"

"Sure. Sounds good."

Her brother put some change in the old pop machine and pulled out a bottle for her.

"So, what did you want to talk to me about?" Gil slipped into a chair beside her and slid the bottle across to her.

"I need a place to store the merchandise from my shop until I can find a new location. Mr. Potter sold the building."

"The new owner won't lease to you?"

Her heart beat a jagged tune and she fought to stay calm. "He said no."

"I'm sorry. When do you have to be out?"

"A couple of weeks." She popped the tab on the can.

"That soon? That doesn't give you much time. Of course you can store your stuff here. Where are you and the boys going to live? You should move in with me until you find a place."

"Gil, I don't think you know what you're offering when you say move in for a bit. The boys are... well, loud, full of energy and... well, boys."

"I've been around them enough to know that," Gil said dryly.

"It's different being around them and living with them." Bella sighed. "It's all happening so fast. I don't know what to do."

"Okay, it's decided. You and the boys will move in with me. I have all that space in the house. Well, the rooms are a bit torn up right now with the remodel, but we'll make it work. You can have your old room back."

She knew that her brother had moved into their parents' house, but it was his home now. She looked across the table at her brother, unable to make a decision.

"Look, I know you don't like to accept help. Let me do this for you. It will only be temporary. Until you get the shop opened somewhere and get back on your feet."

"I hate to impose on you."

It's not an imposition. We're family. I know you like to go it alone, but say yes to help this time."

"Yes." Bella wasn't happy moving in with Gil, but didn't know what else to do. She had to have a place for the boys to live. They'd probably be thrilled to move in with their uncle. "Thanks, Gil."

"You could sound a bit happier about it. And I love to cook, unlike you, little sister." He grinned at her.

"Okay, but it's just temporary. But if you're cooking, can you make your lasagna? Oh, and your meatloaf. Oh —"

"Got it. You move in and we'll have all your favorite foods. I'll make you fat. It'll be great."

"Really, Gil. I appreciate it. I'll try to find us other living arrangements as soon as I can."

"No rush. Now how about I go with you to the ballpark? I hear the boys have games tonight." Gil rose from his chair.

"Sounds good. Want to walk to the park? It's really nice out." She could use the exercise and a few minutes to unwind.

"Yep, just let me lock up the store."

They walked outside and Gil turned to lock the door. A light breeze blew, chasing a bit of her earlier panic away as the wind drifted past her. Things were still a mess, but at least she had a place to live and a place to store her shop merchandise. Now, all she had to do was find a new storefront and a new home. The panic began to creep back, but she pushed it firmly aside.

"You okay?" Gil looked down at her.

"I'm fine. I will be."

"I know you will, Bella. You always are, no matter what life throws at you."

She wished that were true. She would work her way through this and sort out the new store and new place to live. The one thing she didn't know how to sort out was her feelings for Owen. The man she should hate since he was callously tossing her and the boys out, with no regard for the implications it would have on their lives. The man she was so angry with. But also the man with the brown eyes the color of richly-stained walnut. The man with the kisses she couldn't erase from her mind. *Yes, that man.*

Chapter Ten

"Hi Keely." Bella walked into Magnolia Cafe and said hello to the owner. Becky Lee was due to be off soon and they were going to grab some lunch.

"Hi, Bella. Just grab any table. Becky Lee said you were coming in at the end of her shift. She's just checking out her last customer."

"Okay, thanks." Bella took a table by the window. She looked outside at Main Street. Another nice sunny day. A handful of tourists walked down the sidewalks on this Friday afternoon. It would probably be a busy weekend, which was good. She'd like another decent week of sales before she had to close down and store her merchandise. So far, she had only found one spot to lease on Main Street, and it was tiny with no character. It also was double what she paid now. She was probably going to have to move off Main Street and she hated that.

She was going to look on Rosewood Avenue. The area

was starting to have a resurgence of shops. A handful of old Victorian houses had been converted to retail space. Maybe she could find something there. Something with more reasonable rent. It was a pretty area with a cobblestone street, divided by a tree lined median. If she could get a place near the corner of Rosewood Avenue and Main Street, maybe that would work.

"Hey, Izz." Becky Lee dropped into the chair across from her. "You doing okay?"

"Yes, I'm okay." She was going to be okay. Just a lot of changes. She dreaded telling the boys they would have to move. It seemed like they had all just fallen into a good routine with the apartment above the shop. It was easy to keep an eye and an ear on them. Maybe she'd have to hire a high school girl to watch them now. She just didn't think they were old enough to be on their own. Not nearly. But that would be one more expense. It was going to be quite a while until she was back feeling financially stable.

"I've been asking around about a place for you to live. No luck so far."

"I talked to Gil yesterday. I think we're going to move in with him until I can find us somewhere to live." Izzy tried to keep her disappointment out of her voice.

"Oh, Izz. That's a good idea. It gives you more time to get things sorted out. I bet the boys will love it too."

"I'm pretty sure they'll drive Gil crazy within a few days. He's so used to his bachelor lifestyle." Bella sighed.

"I guess I'm lucky he still has our parents' house. It's certainly big enough for all of us. I'll stay in my old room. That will be weird. The boys can stay in Gil's old room. He's in the master bedroom now."

"It will work fine until you can find your own place. Gil's always at the Feed and Seed anyway."

Bella had a hard time looking at the sympathy—or was it pity—in Becky Lee's eyes. She didn't want people to feel sorry for her. She just wanted to sort it all out and get things fixed.

Becky Lee pushed some flyaway strands of her blonde hair back from her face. She always wore her hair pulled back while she worked, but, wow, when she let it down she turned heads. Becky Lee seemed oblivious to her good looks. She dated off and on, but no one serious in quite a few years. Bella had always thought that Becky Lee would have been the first of them to get married, and yet here she was, single. She always seemed happy with her life though.

Bella thought she should grab some of Becky Lee's happy with life attitude. Even though things were up in the air, she had a place to live. She'd find a place for the shop. It would all work out.

"Hey, look who's out there." Becky Lee nodded her head towards the window.

Bella looked out the window and saw Owen walking down the sidewalk on the other side of the street. "Hope he isn't coming here to eat." She tracked his steps.

"I don't think he'd have enough nerve. He probably wants to avoid me, though if he does show up, I have some choice words for the man." Becky Lee reached down and untied her waitress apron and placed it on the table. She stood up. "I'm officially off duty. Let me get us some coffee and brownies. Cook just made a batch and they're still hot."

Bella nodded. She looked out the window and saw Owen head off down the street. Her shoulders relaxed and she took a deep breath. She wasn't ready to see him again. She was so unsure of her feelings. Though how could she like a man who threw her out of her business and home in the pursuit of gain for himself? Well, she didn't like him. She'd just had a momentary fling, no emotional connection. *None. At all.*

Maybe he'd just head back to Chicago now that the deal was made with Mr. Potter. But why did that thought cause her to momentarily feel lost? Too much was going on right now for her to work through any of her thoughts or emotions. Just take one step at a time. Move. Find a place for the shop. Open the new shop. Find a place to live. Don't think about Owen. A list. She should make a list. And put the don't-think-about-Owen as number one on the list.

* * * * *

Becky Lee sat and sipped on her coffee long after Izzy headed back to work. She felt sorry for her friend and hoped she'd be able to do something to make things easier on her. So far, she hadn't had much luck.

Keely came over to her table. "I heard that Bella's building was sold and we're getting a new restaurant in town. Sylvia Landry is going to open her restaurant up again."

"No, really? I knew Owen bought the building, but he's leasing it to Sylvia? That makes no sense. Why? I thought I heard that Sylvia and Jake were in a hard way from all of Sylvia's medical bills."

"I don't know the details, just that Sylvia's is opening back up. It will mean more competition for the cafe. I guess I shouldn't complain. I, at least, still have my business. Is Bella having any luck finding new space for her shop?"

"Not yet." Becky Lee sighed. "Property rentals have really gone up in the last few years. She has to find somewhere for her and the boys to live now too."

"That's a lot to sort through and figure out. I hope she can find a property with reasonable rent for her shop. I'm just lucky my parents bought this building so many years ago. We probably couldn't afford to pay what it would cost to lease a building like this now."

"Well, it's good for the town that things are picking up again. The schools here are bursting at the seams, not to mention the private school. There's such a fine line between sleepy small town and dying small town. I'm glad we're not on the dying side, but things sure are changing. I hope Comfort Crossing keeps its small-town feel."

"Well, business has sure picked up at the cafe. I'm thinking of hiring another waitress for the weekend crowds. Jenny told me about a high school girl that is a hard worker and really needs work. I think I'll talk to her."

Becky Lee smiled. Keely had such a big heart. Always trying to help people. Making a success out of Magnolia Cafe even though the business had kind of been thrust upon her when her father had died. "Sounds good. I'm sure it will only get busier this summer."

"Well, I'm going to go see how things are coming along for the dinner crowd. The cook has been making a new kind of honey yeast roll I think I'll try." Keely walked away toward the kitchen.

Becky Lee sipped on her coffee, lost in thought. She remembered when she had first started working here for Keely's father. She'd been in high school, too. She had worked long hours, always paying her own way for clothes, extra things for school, and eventually buying her own car.

She had grown up with a handful of siblings and not enough money to go around. But what their lives had lacked in things had been more than made up for with love and lots of laughter.

She had saved up money. Then with a bit of inheritance from her aunt—an aunt she hadn't even known she had—Becky Lee had bought the cottage she lived in. The whole long-lost-aunt thing had been strange, but her father never had talked about his sister and refused to talk about her after her death.

Becky Lee had been grateful for the bit of money her aunt had divided between all the siblings. But the haunted look in her father's eyes when he heard of his sister's death still remained permanently etched in her memory.

Becky Lee chased away the memories and took another sip of coffee. She liked working here at the cafe. Maybe some of the townsfolk thought it strange that she would keep one job for so long, but she really enjoyed it. She made enough to cover her expenses, and had enough time off for her favorite hobbies, baking and knitting.

That reminded her. She needed to get over to the Sweet Tea and have Rebecca look at a lace wrap she was knitting. She kept ripping out the last two rows of knitting, and couldn't figure out where she was going wrong. Rebecca was a whiz at knitting and had helped her out before.

Her thoughts bounced from one thing to the next. She put down her coffee cup and slowly got up from the table. She'd walk the short walk home to her cottage and then she thought she'd try baking the new recipe she had found for lasagna without noodles. It used thinly sliced zucchini instead. A person could never have enough uses for zucchini. She grew zucchini, tomatoes, green beans, peppers, and a handful of herbs in her garden each summer. A small garden, but she enjoyed it.

"Bye, Keely." She waved to the woman as she sat at the counter eating one of the new yeast rolls.

Becky Lee pushed out into the sunshine and started her leisurely stroll home. She loved living so near to work. She rarely got her car out anymore, at least not when the weather was nice. It took just over ten minutes or so, at an unhurried pace, to reach her cottage. A perfect distance. The heady scent of gardenia wafted past her as she turned the corner to her street.

She loved her cottage. It was small, two bedrooms, one bath, a front room and the kitchen. But she loved it. She had decorated it with help from Izzy, of course. Her friend knew how to put the most interesting things together, things Becky Lee would never had dreamed would work together. Izzy might be jealous of her cooking ability, but Becky Lee was jealous of Izzy's sense of decorating and style.

Which brought her back to her friend's problems. What were they going to do to help her find a new shop and new place to live? Without really seeming to help, of course, because Izzy liked to solve her own problems these days.

Chapter Eleven

Jeremy and Timmy came bursting through the front door of the shop late Friday afternoon.

"It's not true." Timmy shook his head. "You're a liar."

"Am not."

"Are too."

Timmy ran up to the counter where Bella was going through sales receipts.

"Mom, Jeremy said there's going to be a restaurant here in this building. That's not right, is it? We live here. Your store's here."

Bella had been dreading talking to the boys about moving, but this is not how she had planned to tell them.

"I heard the kids talking at school. It's going to be a restaurant again."

"I hadn't heard it was going to be a restaurant again, but the building has been sold."

A restaurant? Why would Owen buy it and turn it into

a restaurant? It made no sense.

"Why didn't you tell us?" Jeremy's eyes flashed, full of anger.

"I was going to tell you after you got back from your father's this weekend." She sure hadn't wanted to upset them right before they left. "Let's go upstairs and talk."

Bella had underestimated the power of small-town communication. She should have told the boys right away. She asked her part-time helper to watch the store, and led the boys up to the apartment. The boys slid into chairs at the kitchen table. Timmy looked near tears and Jeremy glared at her.

"The building has been sold. We're going to have to move."

"Again? You're making us move again?" Jeremy voice held barely contained aggravation. "We just moved here. You made me share a room with Timmy. Will I at least have my own room when we move?"

"I don't know where we'll live permanently, but for a while we're going to move in with Uncle Gil. You two will have to share Gil's old room."

"I don't want to share a room. We have our own rooms at Dad's." Jeremy's eyes flashed with anger.

"I know this isn't what you want, but it's what we have to deal with. I'm going to have to move the store, too."

"I think living with Uncle Gil will be cool." Timmy looked up at her and she smiled at him.

"Shut up, Timmy. You don't know what you're talking

about."

"Jeremy Hardy. You will not talk to your brother that way. Or to anyone. We don't say shut up. Tell him you're sorry."

"Sorry."

Not even a bit of truthfulness came through but she didn't want to get into an argument on manners right now.

"I know there's been a lot of changes for you boys in the last few years. For all of us. I'm sorry. I know it's been a lot to deal with." She reached for Jeremy's hand, but he snatched it away. She wished she could make things easier for the boys.

"So, by the end of the month we'll move to Gil's. I'll look for a new place for us to live and a new place to open the store. I'm going to bring up some boxes from the store and you can start packing your things when you get back from your dad's."

"Can I take all my stuff?" Timmy asked.

"Of course, sweetheart."

"I think this is stupid. I'm tired of moving. I'm tired of going back and forth all the time." Jeremy scuffed his feet on the floor.

She knew he hated change. He always had. She felt sorry that she had to uproot him again, but it was just the hand they had been dealt. "Jeremy, it's just for a little while. I'll try to find us a place that we can live in for a long time."

"Right."

"Jeremy, I know you're upset, but don't use that tone with me. I'm doing the best I can. I love you guys no matter where we live."

"I love you too, Momma." Timmy reached over and grabbed her hand. "Can we move to Uncle Gil's right away?"

"By the end of the month."

She heard a horn beep out back. Rick must be here to pick up the boys.

"That's your dad. Go get your stuff. I hope you have a great weekend."

"We will, Momma." Timmy hurried off to get his backpack.

"I will. I'll have my own room at Dad's and won't have to share it with Timmy." Jeremy flung the words at her, and left to get his things.

Timmy gave her a big hug before he went clambering down the stairs. Jeremy left in stony silence.

She sat at the table, unwilling to move. Tired. Very tired. Worried about Jeremy being so unhappy, but knowing it was a life lesson that had to be learned. Life throws curves sometimes, like his parents getting divorced, and now having to move again. She'd have to help smooth things over with him during the transition.

She pushed up from the table and cleared some dishes that were still out from breakfast. They'd been running late this morning, and she hadn't even had time to clean up the morning mess. She tidied up the family room area off the kitchen. This apartment was small, but it had been just fine for her and the boys. She was going to miss it.

The phone rang and she went to pick it up after the third ring.

"What's this I hear about you moving the boys again?"

"Hi, Rick." That hadn't taken long.

"Don't you think they've had enough change in their lives?"

Rick had evidently and conveniently forgotten that he was the one who had asked for the divorce.

"The building was sold. I'm going to have to move."

"What are you going to do about the shop?"

She didn't owe him an explanation. "I'll figure it out."

"I told you that you'd never make a go of that shop."

He had told her. Repeatedly. But she had made a go of it. She had been successful. It's just that everything was messed up now.

"I'm sure you don't have enough money to start over."

"Rick, it's my problem, not yours."

"If you're going to play with that shop hobby of yours again, I'm not giving you any money." Rick's angry voice came over the phone lines.

"I didn't ask you too." *Jerk.* Then just as quickly she heard herself chastise herself.

Don't call people names.

She felt guilty even when he deserved it.

"If you can't provide a stable environment for the

boys, then maybe we'll have to revisit our whole custody arrangement."

"Don't be like that, Rick." Her heart began to pound. It was just like him to start stirring up trouble if she didn't do as he wished. He was trying to control her life again, like he had done when they were married. Surely they couldn't take the boys away from her just for moving?

"I think they'd be better off staying with me full time."

She sank down into the chair. Her pulse pounded in her ears, making it hard to hear him. "No, they wouldn't. We're talking about a move here, Rick. A move. Kids move all the time."

"Well, Jeremy isn't happy. I don't think all this upheaval is good, especially for him."

She'd had enough. "Rick, remember you are the one who wanted the divorce. You started us all down this road. I'll get it sorted out. You no longer have a say in how or where I live my life. I'm not moving the boys away from you. We'll still be in town. It's my decision where we live and what I do for a living."

"I might talk to my lawyer."

She wondered if he really was worried about change for the boys, or more that he wanted to have his finger on her again, have some control over her.

"Rick, the building has been sold. We have to move. I'll find us a place to live soon. In the meantime, we'll live at Gil's."

"I knew you wouldn't be able to support the boys with

that ridiculous store of yours."

"Thanks for voicing your opinion, Rick. I've got to go now." She was barely holding onto her temper and she didn't want to start into a big fight with Rick. She had thought they were way past that. Evidently, not so much.

"I mean it. I'm going to talk to my lawyer."

Bella hung up the phone and walked over to the window, looking out over the parking lot behind her building. The sun had tucked behind the clouds and it looked like a storm was coming in. It fit her thunderous mood just fine. The thing was, she had no money to pay a lawyer to fight Rick if he did actually take her back to court. Would a judge really take her boys away? She didn't really trust the legal system, a person never knew what could happen. She couldn't imagine a judge would take them away, but what if Jeremy said he wanted to live with Rick? What if he persuaded Timmy to say it, too? What would happen then? What if she didn't have the shop back up and running and Rick said she couldn't support the boys?

All these questions raced through her mind. She held onto the window sill for support. Her boys. She couldn't handle it if her boys were taken away from her. Her arms ached to hold them right then. To see Jeremy's tousled hair. To hear Timmy's laugh. Heck, she'd be glad to hear them bickering right now.

Maybe she should give up her dream of the shop and just take a job somewhere. Anywhere. Just to have an income. Her heart pounded in her chest, followed quickly by anger. Anger that Rick could still have this kind of control over her life. That he was still pulling strings on her life. But realizing that if it came down to it, she'd take any nine to five job she could get if it meant keeping her boys.

How could her hard work and well planned life have fallen apart in so few days? Her breath quickened and she fought back the 'what ifs' with little success.

Panic swelled through her. Not only had Owen taken her shop and her place to live, he might have managed to get her boys taken away from her, too.

* * * * *

Owen woke up early on Saturday. He had to talk to Izzy —Isabella—Bella. Bella, he loved that name. It fit her so well. He now realized it was just Jenny and Becky Lee who he had heard call her Izzy. The rest of the town called her Bella. He let the unfamiliar name roll off his tongue. He liked the way it sounded. The Izzy he knew was melting into this Bella he was learning about. A successful business woman. A great mom. She was championed by two life-long friends. He could only imagine having friends like that for so many years.

He shook his head. He had brought her world crashing down around her. He'd thought, as he'd gotten closer to Izzy—Bella—that he might finally have a chance to belong somewhere. Here in this town where his brother lived. Where Bella lived. The town had been friendly—friendlier than his brother for that matter—and Bella had been a delightful surprise. He watched in wonder at her easy friendship with Becky Lee and the way she seemed to effortlessly manage her boys. Which, he was sure, wasn't how it really was. Those boys had to be a handful. He didn't know how she did it all.

Rebecca had told him more about Bella when he got back to the Sweet Tea last night. Not in a gossipy way, but in a friendly known-her-all-her-life way. He'd found out that her ex had left her for his new wife. She had built up Bella's Vintage Shop from scratch, with a bit of money from her brother for her half of the family home he had moved into, and a lot of hard work. He admired how she had taken a difficult situation and worked it out.

He actually, for the first time in his business career, wished his deal with Mr. Potter hadn't worked out. Well, not really, because Sylvia deserved having her building and her business back. It was that particular building that held her history. She deserved that and more after the horrible rejection his father had thrown at Sylvia and Jake.

But he felt terrible about ruining the well-earned life that Izzy had built for herself.

Izzy. Isabella. Izzy. Bella. The names whirled through his mind.

Owen sighed at the shambles he had made of her life. He couldn't back out now though. He had promised the building to Sylvia and Jake. He ran his hand through his hair and let out a whoosh of air.

He had to talk to Bella. With a start he realized he had thought of her as Bella, not Izzy. Everything was changing.

He needed to explain things to Bella, but he didn't know how he would do that since he had promised Jake that he wouldn't tell anyone they were brothers. So he had no way to explain to Bella why he had bought her building, why he needed that particular building. But he was going to attempt to smooth things over between them. He had to try.

Owen looked at his watch a couple of dozen times, waiting for it to be time for Bella's Vintage Shop to open. He was at the shop, just moments after she opened the door. She looked up when he came through the doorway. Her face switched from welcoming to what he would peg as panic. She clenched the stack of papers she held in her hand, then looked down and carefully set them on the counter, smoothing them out a bit without much luck.

He crossed the distance between them. The air crackled with tension. When he made it over to the counter, he reached out and stilled her hand that was trying to flatten the receipts. "Bella, can we talk?"

If she had noticed the change from Izzy to Bella, she made no comment, she just nodded at him.

"I'm so sorry about all this. I didn't realize I'd be throwing you out of your store and your home. I wish you'd let me help you find somewhere for the shop, and somewhere to live."

"I don't need you feeling sorry for me. You made it quite clear that it's just business to you."

Her words stung.

He'd sin to be able to explain to her that he did it because he owed his brother. He owed him the building and so much more. He'd promised it was Jake's secret to tell or not, but he really hadn't stopped to consider how it would affect who was leasing it now. "To be honest, I didn't really think about the current tenant. I just assumed they'd move on to another spot."

"How nice and cold-hearted of you." Her eyes flashed in emerald green anger.

"It was cold. Unforgivable. But that doesn't help us with the turmoil I've made of your life. You have to let me help you."

He saw her shoulders straighten and she pulled herself up to her full height. "I don't have to do anything you say."

He lowered his voice and came as close to pleading as he ever had, "Please let me help you."

"Owen, I can't. I need to figure this out by myself."

"But you would never have been in this predicament if I hadn't bought the building."

"It's all just 'what ifs'. But we have what we have now."

"I am truly sorry for all the pain and upheaval I've caused." He was sorry. He had never deliberately hurt a person in his life. At least he didn't think he had.

"Owen, I need to get to work. I appreciate your apology. I believe you when you said you didn't know it was me owning the shop."

"I didn't know."

She just nodded at him with sad eyes and the look of the weight of the world upon her shoulders. The shoulders with waves of golden red hair flowing over them. How he wanted to take her in his arms and just make things better. Fix things for her. That's what he did. Fixed things. Made deals and smoothed the way to better profits for the companies he bought.

He just couldn't find a way to smooth the way for Bella.

Or could he?

* * * * *

Owen hurried down Main Street full of ideas. Maybe he could pull this off. Maybe he could actually help. Then, there would be the problem of Bella accepting any help. He'd need a way for it to sound like she was helping him. No, he needed to find a way that fixed things and benefitted both of them for Bella to accept help. He could do that. He was good at sorting out problems and figuring out impossible situations. This time he'd use his skill for a high stakes game. He wanted to make Bella happy and make her life easier.

Oh, what the heck, he longed for her to want to date him again. He wanted to kiss her and see her satisfied sexy smile after he kissed her. He'd do everything in his power to see that smile even one more time.

He walked past the park. He loved the idea of a town park right on Main Street where people could gather and picnic or play. He also knew it was the center of the handful of festivals they had each year. The town was really growing on him. He had held out, false hopes now, that he would begin to fit in here. Between Bella's anger and the fact that Jake could barely stand to be in the same room with him, things weren't looking good for finding a place to call home, even if it was only for brief periods of time. He was also pretty sure that by throwing Bella out of her home, he had made his fair share of enemies in the town. That thought displeased him. A lot. He wanted the people of the town to like him, maybe even accept him. He wanted *Jake* to accept him and call him his brother. He wanted Bella to forgive him, really forgive him and go out with him again and see where it led.

As if the universe was listening, he noticed Bella's boys playing near the swings in the park. Freely admitting to himself he wasn't good with kids, he decided to go say hi to them. He crossed the grass and walked over to where they were playing. "Hi, boys."

Both of the boys looked up at him. "Hi." Jeremy didn't sound happy to see him. Owen looked hopefully at Timmy. The boy had always seemed to like him.

"Hi." Timmy looked up at his accusingly. "You're the

one who made my mom sad. My dad said you bought the building we live in and you're throwing us out."

"Ah, Timmy, it's not exactly like that." Though, to be honest, it was exactly like that. It was beyond him to explain a business deal and how things worked in the real world to the boys. He had no experience talking to kids. He couldn't explain he had done it to help his brother. That wasn't his secret to tell.

"Yeah, and now Dad says we need to live with him because Mom doesn't have a... stable 'vironment for us to live in. We might have to talk to a judge and everything." Jeremy's eyes flashed with a mirror anger of Bella's.

"What?"

"Dad said Momma can't support us. She's not going to make any money with her shop closed. So, we'll have to live with him. I don't want to. I love my momma." Timmy was near tears.

Owen's heart dropped in his chest. He was out of his element. He didn't know how to make the boys feel better. He wanted to promise them both that it would all work out. Only, of course, he didn't know that.

Jeremy put his arm protectively around his little brother. "Don't cry, Timmy. We'll still see Mom some."

"But Dad said we'd stay with him all the time. She won't tuck me in at night or anything." Timmy brushed away a tear that ran down his dusty cheek, leaving a trail of hurt in its wake.

The air sucked out of Owen's lungs. He not only had taken Bella's shop and her home, he might have caused her to lose the boys.

That was not going to happen. Not.

Rick walked up to them just then. Owen had to keep from telling Rick what he thought of him. What he thought of him threatening to take the boys away. For talking about their mother like that in front of the boys. He had this unfamiliar urge to stand in front of the boys to protect them from their own father.

Owen felt his jaw clench even as he reached out a hand in greeting. "Rick."

"Owen." There was no warmth or even a hint of glad-to-see-you in Rick's voice.

The feeling is mutual, bud.

"Come on boys, time to go. I'm done with my meeting."

"What did your lawyer say, Dad? Is he going to make me move away from Momma?" Timmy's eyes held a tinge of hope in them. Hope that Rick wouldn't force him to leave his mother.

"We'll talk later, boys."

Rick nodded at Owen, motioned to the boys, and they all three turned and walked away.

Owen stood there watching them walk away, Timmy in tears. Rick sure hadn't wasted any time. Owen was going to halt this train wreck he'd created. An unfamiliar pain ripped through him at seeing Timmy's tears. The feeling punched him in the gut. He had caused this and he would do everything in his power to put a smile back on the little guy's face.

* * * * *

Jenny saw him standing at the edge of the park. Owen. The man who was doing his best to ruin one of her best friends. She picked up her pace and stalked over to where he stood looking off down the street, obviously lost in thought.

"Mr. Campbell." She interrupted his thoughts.

"Yes, Mrs. Bouchard. I met you at Bella's shop." The man had an almost guilty look on his face.

Good. He should feel guilty. "I thought you would have left town by now."

"I'm staying to oversee the start of the rehabbing of the building. It shouldn't take too long."

"It would be easier for Izzy if you left town." Jenny was in no mood to mince words with the man, the man who was making Izzy's life so difficult right now.

"It probably would be." Owen nodded. "But, I'm not leaving. I'm actually trying to figure something out. A way to help Bella."

"I doubt if she'll take any help from you." If Izzy wouldn't take help from her, she sure wouldn't take help from Owen.

"I know she's proud of all she's accomplished and how successful she's made her store. She has a right to be. It's a lot of hard work to open a business like that."

"It was very hard. Now, you're taking all that away from her."

"I didn't mean to. But, that's no excuse, really. I'm going to fix this mess I made of her life."

Jenny eyed the man suspiciously. "What do you mean, fix it? Izzy doesn't really like people to fix things for her or tell her what she should do."

"I've gathered that from the short time I've known her. I'd like to come up with a solution that benefits both of us." Owen raked his hand through his hair. "I've got a couple of ideas. I have my business team looking into a few things for me."

"Just what are you planning?"

"I know she won't take outright help, so I'm working on something that will help both of us. Her business and my business."

"Well, if you can pull that off, then maybe I'll quit thinking you're such a scoundrel."

"Scoundrel? Do people really use that word any more?" Owen smiled at her.

"Well, it seems to fit you. Unless, of course, you figure a way out of this mess you made." Jenny was beginning to have hope for her friend.

"I care about Bella. I know we just met, but she has... I don't know... touched my life in a way I wasn't expecting." Owen's face held an almost sheepish expression.

Jenny was good at reading people, and right now she'd

say that Owen Campbell was actually smitten with Izzy. She could see it in his eyes when he talked about her. Which was good, because she knew Izzy had feelings for Owen, whether she'd admit it or not. If they could find a way out of this mess, maybe there was some hope for the two of them.

"I hope you can figure something out. I'll help in any way I can. Jenny pinned him with a listen-to-me look. "But, Owen, don't hurt her again."

"I'll do my best. I promise. I'm going to try and make things right."

Chapter Twelve

Bella was determined not to spend the evening talking about her troubles. Becky Lee had invited her and Jenny over for dinner. She wanted nothing more than an escape from… well, everything.

She knocked on the screen door to Becky Lee's cottage and went on inside. "Bec, I'm here."

"In the kitchen. Come on back."

Bella crossed through the front room and into the short hallway to the kitchen. Jenny sat at the kitchen table while Becky Lee was stirring something at the stove.

"Hey, Izzy. Want some iced sweet tea?" Becky Lee motioned to a big pitcher on the table.

"Sounds great." Bella sank into a chair at the table. "What are you cooking? It smells wonderful."

"Gumbo. And we're going to have a nice salad with it. Strawberry vinaigrette dressing. Then I made you that strawberry pie that you like so much."

"You spoil me, Bec."

"I'm trying. Besides, you know I love having people over to cook for."

"You counting down the days until school is out?" Bella turned to Jenny.

"I am. Almost over. And it looks like Nathan has pulled his grades up enough that there won't be summer school in our future. Hoping for a slow, lazy summer."

"That's great news." Bella took a sip of the tea. Becky Lee even made the best tea in town.

"Any luck on finding a place for the shop?" Jenny asked.

So much for not thinking about her problems tonight, but of course her friends would ask about it. "Not yet."

"The offer still stands to lend you some money if you need it." Jenny looked across the table directly at Bella. "No strings."

"Thank you, but, no thanks."

"You know, Izzy, it's okay to accept help. None of us make it through this life without a little help from our friends," Becky Lee added.

Her friends were right. She could accept help, it would make things so much easier. But she really wanted to do this on her own. Maybe it was pride. Maybe it was stubbornness. Maybe it was foolish.

"You do what you think is best. You know we're behind you one hundred percent." Jenny said.

"I really do appreciate the offer. Really. Maybe I

should just get a job for a while. Rick is threatening to take the boys away because I don't have an income to support them."

"He can't do that. Rick is a selfish jerk. He just wants to control you. He never liked that you opened your shop." Becky Lee crossed over and sat beside Bella. "There is no way a judge would take those boys away."

"I could talk to Joseph's father, William, about it. Maybe get someone in his law firm to work with you?"

"I don't have the money to fight Rick in court. It would be easier to just get a regular job, so he doesn't have the whole she-is-worthless-doesn't-make-money thing." Bella sighed. It scared her witless to think of going back to court. She thought that was so behind her, the bickering over custody, all of that.

"You are not worthless and don't let Rick beat you down again. You are not going to get a regular job. The shop is your life now. You love it. It has made you just come alive." Jenny's eyes flashed with anger. "Rick is just being Rick. At least he never disappoints us these days… he's always a jerk."

"I can't risk losing the boys. I just can't." Bella blinked, trying to fight back the tears that seemed to hover right on the edge for the last week. She was not going to break down in front of her friends. She wasn't.

"We're not going to let Rick do this to you. I'm going to talk to William and see what he recommends. We'll worry about paying for a lawyer later, let's just get some legal advice. William won't charge for talking to me about this. Let me do this for you." Jenny said.

Bella nodded. She'd get over her pride and accept help if it meant keeping the boys. She'd do anything for them. Even get a full time regular job.

"Jenny is right. We'll sort this out. This is Rick rattling his cage. He does that so well. He just wants to scare you into doing what he wants you to do. Classic Rick. Let Jenny talk to William." Becky Lee put her hand on Bella's.

Bella looked at her two friends. Life-long friends. The ones who were always there for her. How did she get so lucky? Some people go through their whole lives without even one friend as special as Jenny and Becky Lee.

"I love you guys." Bella felt the tears recede. "Thanks for always being there for me."

"There is no place we'd rather be." Becky Lee wrapped her arm around Bella and squeezed. "The three of us can get through anything life throws at us."

* * * * *

Owen had accepted Sylvia's invitation to dinner. He hoped Jake was okay with him coming over. Sylvia had said her sister was out of town for a few days, and she had taken over the kitchen, trying out new recipes. She was going to do a sampler dinner of some of the dishes she was thinking of putting on the menu.

He arrived promptly at six, with a bottle of wine in his hand. Sylvia answered the door with flushed cheeks and an apron dusted with flour.

"Come in. Come on back to the kitchen. I'm just finishing up a few things. Jake is out. He should be back any minute."

Or maybe Jake was planning on just not coming home after he had heard that Sylvia had invited him over. Owen wouldn't be surprised. He followed Sylvia to the kitchen. Jake was coming in the back door as they got to the kitchen. Okay, so he was going to join them.

"I brought some wine." Owen held up the bottle.

"My mother doesn't drink."

"Oh, well…" Owen shifted back and forth, lowering the bottle of wine. Another screw up on his part.

"Actually, I'd love to try your wine." Sylvia turned, opened a cabinet, and took out three wine glasses. "You going to join us, Jake?"

"I'll stick with a beer." Jake walked to the fridge, pulled out a can of beer, and popped the top. He lounged against the counter, eyeing Owen.

"I know my sister has a wine opener somewhere. Can you look in that drawer behind you, Owen?"

Owen did as he was told and rooted through a drawer full of spatulas, slotted spoons, a can opener, some bag clips, and who knew what else. He triumphantly held up the wine opener. "Got it."

"Will you open the wine?" Sylvia asked.

"Sure thing." Owen opened the bottle, poured two glasses, and handed one to Sylvia.

The woman took a sip and smiled. "Nice. It's been a long time since I've had wine. Totally gave up alcohol with the cancer scare. I don't think a nice glass of red wine is going to hurt anything now."

Owen didn't know what to say. He didn't know what kind of cancer Sylvia had had, only that it had taken her a few years to get back on her feet. She looked healthy enough to him. Thin, but good color. She looked happy here in the kitchen, messing with things on the stove and peeking into the oven.

"You two boys sit down. I'll have dinner on the table in a jiffy."

Owen wasn't sure the last time he had been called a boy, but once again he did as he was told and sat at the table. Jake took the seat across from him and settled his beer on the table.

Sylvia set down an array of dishes in front of them, then took her place at the head of the table. "Hope you like these. Let me know what you think of each one. I've been busy working on the new menu."

Owen thought every single dish that Sylvia made was wonderful. She was a fabulous cook, which he told her at least a half dozen times as he sampled the dishes.

Jake ate in silence.

Sylvia finally turned to her son. "Jake, I expect you to be polite to our guest. He is your brother. Nothing your father did is Owen's fault. I know you aren't happy that I accepted his offer of the building and help opening the restaurant, but it is something I really want. I accepted the fact that Stephen wasn't going to have anything to do with you, nor was he going to help support you. But he should have. It was just as much his responsibility as it was mine."

Sylvia then turned to Owen. "I didn't know that Stephen was married when I was seeing him. He didn't tell me he was and he wore no wedding ring. I don't want you to think I was some kind of homewrecker. Not that I wrecked his home, since he just walked away from us."

"I'm very sorry he did that."

"The man missed out. His loss for not having the joy of Jake in his life."

"Jake didn't miss much not having our father, well, as a father. He was cold and totally uninterested in my life except for grades. He was rarely around. Neither was my mother." Owen put down his silverware.

"So you want me to feel sorry for you?" Jake glared at Owen.

"No, I want you to know that I think you got a better deal with your family all around you and a mother who obviously cares about you. No amount of money can buy that. You are one lucky man."

* * * * *

Jake knew his mother was right. He was being a jerk. Owen was right, too. He was a lucky man. He'd had everything he needed growing up. They hadn't had much money, but they'd gotten by. The family had helped him out so much the last few years, too. He'd been busy working two jobs to try and pay the bills. The family had helped take care of his mother, sat with her during chemotherapy treatments when he couldn't, and brought food when she had been too tired to grocery shop or cook.

"Owen, I'm sorry. I've been behaving like a jerk."

"Apology accepted."

"I still don't want anything from our father, but my mother deserves it. She had no help from the man, no support at all. If she wants the family building back and wants to open up her restaurant again, then I'm happy you could do that for her."

"I'm glad I could do it for both of you."

"I know I'm late in saying this, but thank you. I do appreciate you making my mama so happy."

His mother smiled. "That's better. I was hoping you two could become friends. This is a start."

"So, Mama, now you want to have this fancy menu restaurant. Let me just say that these dishes you cooked tonight were great. If a fancier restaurant is what you want, I'm all for it."

"Thanks, son." Sylvia got up to clear the table.

"Let me help." Owen stood up.

The three of them cleared away the dinner dishes and his mother put out a peach pie, some kind of chocolatey fancy looking thing, and a strawberry tart. He had to admit he'd been eating very well the last week or so with all his mother's experimenting.

They all tried the three desserts, but none of them could agree on which was the best.

"Sylvia, those were so good. I'm going to leave the menu in your capable hands." Owen pushed away from the table. "I have some workers coming at the first of the month to do some rehab work. Going to replace the refrigeration system, too. I'll get you in there straight away and let you check everything out. You can let me know if anything else needs upgrading or needs to be fixed. I thought we could remodel the bathrooms too. I'm hoping to have all the work finished in about a month's time."

"You're doing all that, too?" Jake was surprised his brother was spending even more money on the building.

"If you both agree, yes."

"I think that's wonderful. The old bathrooms were in need of a refresh. You are right that the old refrigerator was on its last legs. I appreciate all that you're doing." His mother folded her napkin and set it on the table. "The one thing I'm not happy with is Bella Amaud. I feel badly that she's losing her shop space and the apartment she lived in. I hear she's having a hard time finding a new space for the shop. I also hear you were seeing her before all this happened."

"Not much is secret in a small town, is it?" Owen smiled. "I'm working on a solution for Bella. I didn't know that Bella was the renter. She's pretty upset with me right now. She thinks it's just a cold, calculated business deal."

"You didn't tell her about us, did you? You promised you wouldn't." Jake looked closely at his brother.

"No, I gave you my word."

"Jake, I don't think it would be wrong for Owen to tell Bella. It might make her understand better, make her not so upset with Owen."

"Mama, I don't want the town talking about you. It's been years since anyone has said a word about who my father might be."

"You have to know I'm at an age where I just don't care if people talk about me, son."

"No. There is no need for anyone to know."

"You don't want people to know that Owen is your brother? Don't you think they'll be curious why he's doing all this for us?"

"It's no one's business but ours."

"I won't say anything, if you still don't want me to." Owen said.

"I don't want you to."

His mother sighed. "You're being stubborn, son."

"No, I'm being a good son and protecting you from gossip."

"I don't really need protecting." His mother got up from the table and cleared away her dessert plate. "I'm perfectly capable of fighting my own battles. Always have been. You know, you've got your father's stubborn streak."

"I'm nothing like my father. Nothing at all."

Chapter Thirteen

Owen spent the next few days working with his business team, trying to come up with a solution to the problems he'd caused for Bella. After a couple of days, he was pleased to find what he thought would be something Bella would agree to. He'd have to approach her carefully, but she seemed to have a good head for figures and he could prove this would be beneficial to both of them.

He sat out on the front porch of the Sweet Tea with his notebook, jotting down notes. He went over the numbers again. Yes, he thought this would work.

Rebecca came out on the porch carrying a tray. "Would you like a glass of sweet tea?"

"Yes, I would. That sounds nice."

Rebecca set the tray on a small table and poured him a glass.

"Care to join me for a bit?" Owen nodded to the chair

beside him. "I could use a break."

"I could, too." Rebecca poured another glass and plopped into the chair beside him. "That was a crazy busy weekend with the full house of guests. I'm still recovering. I'm glad for the business, but if it were like that all the time, I'd hire some more help."

"I don't know how you managed with that crowd and the constant stream for breakfasts each morning—which were delicious, by the way."

"Thanks. I kind of get in the swing of cooking when it's that busy. I try and do part of the breakfast the night before, like bake bread or coffee cake." Rebecca took a sip of her tea and rocked her chair, just a hint of a back and forth motion. Wisps of her grey hair blew in the light breeze.

"I talked to Larry, and told him I would like to stay another week or so. He said that was fine with your schedule" Owen said.

"Yes, that works fine. Business keeping in you in town longer than you thought?"

"That, and I'm trying to undo how I botched up Bella's life."

"That would be nice." Rebecca's voice didn't hold any recrimination, just straight facts.

"I think it's going to work out. But, I'll have to see if Bella agrees to it."

"She's an independent woman these days, but practical. Won't take a handout from you, though."

"I know. I think I came up with something that would benefit both of us."

"You like her, don't you?" Rebecca gave him a look that said she expected honesty.

"I do like her. I like this town. You and Larry have both been so welcoming, too." Owen was surprised to find how easy it was for him to talk to Rebecca.

"To be honest, before this whole deal where I found out I was displacing Bella, I had started to entertain thoughts of being here in Comfort Crossing more often. Getting to know Jake. It's the first place I ever felt that everyone just accepted me for who I am. I didn't have to live up to anyone's expectations. I'm envious of what you all have here. Families. Lifelong friends. I'm tired of feeling like the little kid, outside, looking through the window at all the family fun going on inside. The laughter. Family meals. All of that."

"You don't have that back in Chicago? No family?"

"It's just me."

"I'm sorry. Being alone isn't any way to live life. Life is meant to be shared. With family, with friends, with someone you love."

"I just never thought that kind of life was possible for me. I didn't even realize that I wanted it… though, maybe I guess I always have. I was always envious of the kids whose parents came to all their games, or even of the moms who gave embarrassing kisses to my teammates." Owen took another sip of tea and looked out at the pretty yard in front of the B&B. "I look at the friendship that Bella, Jenny, and Becky Lee have. I want that. Friends I can talk to and just hang out with."

"If that's what you want, you should go after it. Life is too short to spend it on anything but the things that make your heart sing and the people who are important to you."

"I don't know if Bella will even speak to me, much less ever go out with me again."

"You're never going to know unless you try, are you? You lay out your plan for her, and see if she'll agree to it. Then, give her some time and see what happens. Keep trying. Tell her how you feel. It's hard work to make your dreams come true."

* * * * *

"What do you mean Timmy isn't here?" Bella's heart beat with a horrible irregular thumping.

"I thought he was watching TV. I was in our bedroom. Then when I came out to watch TV with him, he wasn't there, so I came downstairs to tell you." Jeremy had a worried look in his eyes. It was his responsibility to keep an eye on his brother when they were upstairs and Bella was down in the shop.

"Did you look outside?" Bella's mind whirled through all the reasons that Timmy wouldn't be upstairs. Upstairs where he was supposed to be.

"He knows we're not allowed to leave without telling you. But I looked out back and he's not there either."

Bella rushed to the front window and looked out on the street. No sign of her son. She stepped outside and scanned Main Street in both directions. Still no Timmy.

Her heart raced and she motioned to Jeremy to join her. Without wasting anymore time, she flipped the sign to say closed. "Come on, let's go look at the park." She locked the store door behind her. It wasn't like Timmy to leave without telling her. He was allowed to play out back of the store, but not go anywhere else on his own. She took a quick breath, refusing to panic just yet. He had probably gone to the park to play with his friends. But she didn't quite believe it. She sucked in a big gulp of air. *Don't panic. Stay clear-headed.*

They quickly walked down the street—just a half pace short of full-out run. They reached the park. No sign of Timmy. She felt herself start to panic, but firmly put it away. *Focus.*

She grabbed Jeremy's hand. "Let's try Magnolia Cafe."

The short walk back to the cafe seemed to take twice as long as it should have. Jeremy struggled to keep up with her pace with his short legs. She hurried into the cafe and scanned the tables. No sign of Timmy.

Becky Lee waved from across the room, finished taking an order, and came up to them. "You guys here to eat?"

"No, we're looking for Timmy. I c-c-can't find him." Bella used every power within her to keep in control. Her heart was racing and she clenched her fists.

171

"Keely, I have to go. Timmy's missing." Becky Lee handed her waitress apron and the order she had just taken to her boss.

"Go. Don't worry about a thing here. I'll keep an eye out the window for him and call you if I see him." Keely took the apron and order.

Becky Lee put her arm around Bella and gave a quick squeeze. "Okay, let's find him."

Bella leaned into Becky Lee, drawing on her strength. "I don't know where else to look."

"Do you think he left something at school?" Jeremy asked.

"I don't know, but that's a good suggestion." Bella turned to Becky Lee. "I'm going to take Jeremy to help me look at the school."

"I'll go look the other direction. I'll ask around some of the shops and see if anyone has seen him." Becky Lee stepped outside with Bella and Jeremy. "I've got my cell. I'll call if I have any news."

Bella nodded then turned and hurried down towards the school, with Jeremy right by her side. Maybe Timmy had left a book at school that he needed for homework and was afraid she'd be mad at him for forgetting? It didn't sound like him, and he knew he wasn't supposed to leave the apartment alone. But it was worth a shot. Her heart beat faster with every step they took.

Jenny was just leaving the school when they came rushing up to the building.

"Jenny, have you seen Timmy?"

"No, why?"

"He's missing. Becky Lee is looking downtown for me. I can't—" The words choked her, threatening to strangle all rational thought. The only reason she was able to keep from breaking into sobs was knowing that wouldn't help her find him.

"Okay, let's search the school. I'll do the lower grades, checking each room. You two do the upper grades." Jenny took charge, which was good because Bella could barely squeeze out a coherent thought, her eyes constantly scanning around her.

Jenny headed back inside and Bella followed her friend. A plan. Jenny had a plan. Someone to tell her where to look. Where to find her son. She swiped at a lone tear that escaped. She didn't have time for that. *Stay focused.*

"Mom, I'm sorry. I was supposed to watch him." Jeremy's face held a scared and forlorn expression.

"Jeremy, we'll talk about that later. You are supposed to watch him, but it's obvious he didn't want you to know he left. I do appreciate you helping me look for him." She gave her son a quick hug. "Let's go look."

They looked in every room and came back to meet Jenny at the front of the school. "No luck?" Bella's face fell as she saw Jenny standing alone.

"I called Becky Lee, but no sign of him yet." Jenny slid her cell phone into her pocket.

"I should call Rick."

"I think you should."

Bella dreaded the call, but knew it was Rick's right to know Timmy was missing. Besides, he could help with the search.

Rick picked up on the second ring.

"If you're calling about my talking to the lawyer about changing the custody arrangement, I think it best to let the lawyers hammer that out." He didn't even give her a chance to say anything. No hello to her. Just a barrage of words. She hated caller id sometimes.

Bella took a deep breath. "Timmy is missing."

"What do you mean missing?"

"I can't find him."

"See, I told you it wasn't working out to have the boys live with you when your life is such a mess." His accusations and anger thundered through the phone. "This is it. When we find him, I'm taking the boys back home with me."

She let him yell at her, because she felt badly enough. Guilty for not keeping a better eye on Timmy. Wondering why he'd left. Rick might as well blame her, because she sure blamed herself. What kind of mother drove her son to run away?

"Where have you looked?" Rick's voice held a cold and accusing tone.

"We've looked at the school, the park, and the cafe."

"I'll be there as soon as I can."

The disconnect of the phone echoed in her ear. She had made a mess of the boys' lives. Planning on moving them to Gil's, knowing they would move again. Closing her shop and not knowing when she could open it again and start earning an income. Timmy running away would be one more piece of ammunition Rick would use to try and take the boys away.

She looked at Jenny, trying to fight back tears. Jenny crossed the distance between them and took Bella into her arms. Bella no longer had the strength to fight back the tears. They came in big, ugly gulps of breath. Her shoulders heaved and she clung tightly to her friend. Jenny held her and let her cry.

Bella finally pulled away and swiped her hands across her face to wipe away the tears. "I can't do this. I need to pull myself together and keep looking."

"Mom, you okay?" Jeremy's small voice sounded scared.

"Yes, I'll be okay." She knelt down and wrapped her arms around her son. "We should get back to looking for Timmy. Do you have any other ideas of where to look?"

"Maybe we should go back home and see if he went there?"

"That's a good idea. Let's go back and look there."

Bella took a deep breath, fighting for control. She was living one of a mother's worst nightmares. She just wished she could wake up from it, everything would be okay, and Timmy would crawl into her lap and hug her.

* * * * *

Owen sat out on the porch of the Sweet Tea long after Rebecca had gone back inside. He liked the privacy of being tucked away on the end of the porch, shielded by a large magnolia tree. It was kind of like having an outside office. That appealed to him, which surprised him. He was used to his glass-walled corner office in downtown Chicago. This was certainly a change for him. While he was used to doing business while he was on the road, it was usually from his hotel room or doing paperwork while he ate somewhere. He'd never had a tree-shielded front porch office.

"Mr. Campbell?"

Owen looked up and saw Timmy standing at the top of the stairs to the porch.

"Timmy, what are you doing here? Is your mom with you?"

"No, my momma's not here. I came all by myself. It's not far."

It was only a handful of blocks from the B&B to the Bella's shop, but Owen was surprised Timmy was allowed to go that far alone. It just went to show how little he knew about raising kids in a small town. Or raising them anywhere for that matter.

Timmy crossed the porch and stood in front of Owen, shuffling one foot back and forth on the worn planks of the porch. "I came to talk to you."

Owen wasn't used to being sought out by children.

"Okay, what do you want to talk about?"

Timmy had such a serious expression on his face. "I want to talk about my mom's shop."

"What about it?"

Timmy looked him straight in the eye. "I want you to not make my momma leave the shop or our apartment."

"I wish I could, Timmy, but I already have plans in place for the building. I've promised it to someone else. I can't go back on my word. I didn't know your mom and you boys lived above the shop."

"But you could buy a different building."

"I need this building. It has to be this one. It just does." Owen could tell that he hadn't explained it very well. He couldn't explain why it needed to be this building, without breaking his promise to Jake. Besides, he really had no idea how to talk to children, how to explain.

"But, if you make Momma leave, then Dad says we have to go live with him all the time. I don't want to."

Owen looked at the boy, unwilling to tell him what a jerk his father was being, but not knowing what to say to make Timmy feel better. "Maybe your mom and dad can work something out."

"Dad already talked to his lawyer. And I heard Momma talking to Miss Jenny. She said she doesn't have money for a lawyer."

"Well, I'll tell you a secret, Timmy. I'm trying to work out something to help your mom, to try and make all this right. But I have a few more things to figure out first. If

everything works, hopefully your father will be happy."
Not that he gave a whit whether Rick was happy or not.
But if he could make it so Rick didn't try and take Bella's
sons from her, that's all he wanted from the man.

Timmy's eyes shone with hope. "You think so? You
think you can fix this?"

"I'm sure going to try."

Rebecca came back out on the porch. "Timmy, what
are you doing here?"

"I came to see Mr. Campbell."

"Does your mother know you're here?"

Timmy looked down at the porch. He gave a big sigh.
"No, Ma'am."

"Well, how about I give her a call while you stay here
with Mr. Campbell. We'll just let her know you're here."

"Okay. But she's going to be mad at me." Timmy
plopped down in the rocker beside Owen.

Owen realized how clueless he'd been. Of course
Timmy was too young to be wandering around by
himself, small town or not. Rebecca had figured that out
immediately. Just add that to one more mistake he'd
made with Bella.

Rebecca hurried back into the B&B.

"So, your mom doesn't know where you are?"

"No, sir."

"Don't you think she's going to be worried?"

"I guess, but I wanted to see if you'd let Momma stay in
her shop and let us live upstairs. I thought maybe I could

fix it for her."

"Well, it looks like you and I are on the same page for that, Timmy my friend. We both want to fix this mess, don't we?"

Owen's phone rang and he listened to his business manager give him the quick details on his plan to help Bella. It looked like all the pieces were in place. "Thanks." He ended the call and slid the cell phone back in his pocket.

"Timmy, looks like we're in luck. I think I have a solution to our problem."

Timmy grinned from ear to ear. "I knew it was a good idea to come talk to you." His small legs swung back and forth from the chair.

Chapter Fourteen

Bella snatched her cell phone out of her pocket and answered on the first ring. "Hello?"

"Izzy. It's Becky Lee. Timmy is fine. He's at the Sweet Tea. Rebecca tried to call your store but when you didn't answer, she called Keely at Magnolia Cafe. Keely called my cell."

Bella's heart leapt and the unbearable weight that had been crushing down on her for the last hour began to lift away. "I'm on my way."

She quickly dialed Rick's number, told him where Timmy was, and hung up before Rick could say a word to her.

A smile grabbed her and wouldn't let go. She turned to Jeremy. "He's at the Sweet Tea. Let's go."

Jeremy grabbed her hand and they ran down the street to the B&B. Within minutes they were in front of the Sweet Tea. Bella took a deep breath to calm herself and climbed the porch stairs. Then she saw Timmy sitting at the end of the porch and tears rushed to her eyes.

"Timmy." She sank to her knees and held out her arms. Timmy came running over and launched himself into her embrace. She held him close, gathering in the sweet scent of his hair, feeling his tears mingle with hers on her cheek. She rocked back and forth, undyingly grateful to have her son in her arms.

Timmy pulled back after a few minutes. "I'm in trouble, aren't I?"

Bella looked right into his eyes. "You're not supposed to leave the apartment alone. You know that."

She gathered him back into her arms, unable to scold him right now, knowing they would have to have a serious discussion at some point.

She looked up and saw Owen standing beside them. "Timmy came to talk to me."

"Really?" Surprise washed over her. "What about?"

Right then Rick pulled up in front of the B&B and took the distance from the car to the porch in a few long strides. "Tim. You okay?"

Timmy nodded. Bella stood up but still held tightly to Timmy's hand.

"Why did you leave your mom's place? Were you upset she's moving you?"

Timmy looked from his mom, to his dad, to Owen. Owen nodded to him. The little boy drew in a large gulp of air.

"I came to see if Mr. Campbell would let Momma stay at the shop and let us stay at the apartment. I don't want to live with you all the time, Dad. Don't be mad at me. But I like being with Momma too. I want to keep going back and forth, not stay all the time with you. I'd miss Momma and she tucks me in better than you do."

Rick looked at his son. "Timmy, sometimes a parent knows what's better for their child than they do."

Jeremy went to stand by Timmy. "Dad, I don't want to live with you all the time either. Even if I do have my own room there."

"Boys, I'm just doing what's best for you until your mom can figure out her life and a place for you to live."

Fear chased through Bella. She held tightly to both Jeremy's hand and Timmy's.

"But we don't want to, Dad." Timmy said.

"It's for a judge to decide." Rick stood firm in his decision. "Come on, boys. You're going to my house tonight."

"It's not our night to go to your house." Jeremy insisted.

Timmy burst into tears and clung to his mother.

"Rick, we're not going to talk about any of this in front of the boys. It's the boys' night to be with me, nothing has changed so far. You need to give me time to sort out where I can move the shop and find a permanent place to live."

Rick stood there, an angry look plastered on his face.

He wasn't used to people not jumping to his bidding. "You've got one week."

Rick turned on his heels and stomped across the yard. There was no other way that Bella could think of to describe Rick's departure. He stomped away like a little boy who hadn't gotten his way. It was never a good idea to not let Rick get his way. It always meant trouble. Bella let a sigh escape.

Rebecca came out of the porch again. "Bella, glad you got the message. It was kind of a tortuous route, but I didn't have your cell phone number."

"Thank you so much for calling."

"So, I thought after all that excitement, the boys might be hungry. How about you two boys come inside? I just made some sugar cookies and I bet they'd go great with a big glass of milk. What do you say?"

"Can we, Mom?" Jeremy asked.

"Sure. That sounds great. Thanks Rebecca."

"You two just sit down and have some more of that sweet tea. We'll be back out in a bit." Rebecca led the boys inside.

"Come on. Let's sit down. You look like a wisp of a breeze could knock you over." Owen walked across the porch and Bella followed.

She sank into the rocking chair and Owen poured her some tea. He held out the glass, and she reached for it, noticing her hands were shaking. Owen's fingers brushed hers as he handed her the glass, and he waited for her hands to steady before letting go of the glass. She took a sip and placed it carefully back on the table.

Just then Sylvia and Jake Landry came walking up the steps to the Sweet Tea.

"Bella, there you are, dear. I was at Magnolia Cafe and heard your son ran away. But you found him, right? I hope we didn't cause all this by us getting the building back." Sylvia crossed over to where Bella was sitting.

"No, it's not your fault. I understand how you'd want the building back. It's been in your family for generations."

"If it's going to cause you this much trouble, then I'll turn down Owen's offer and you can stay there."

"No, I'll be fine. I'll find another spot for the shop. We're going to stay at my brother's until I work out where we'll live."

Owen leaned forward in his chair and touched her leg. "I guess this is as good a time as any to talk to you, Bella. I have a business deal I want to discuss with you. Will you hear me out?"

She looked at Owen, who was watching her with such an intense look in his eyes. She nodded.

"I know you want to do things on your own. I get that. I have a bit of an independent streak myself." He flashed her a wry smile. "Anyway, I've bought two properties on Rosewood Avenue. One on the corner of Main and Rosewood, one across the street and a couple houses down. The houses there are zoned for commercial, as you know. I want to rent the one on the corner of Main and Rosewood to you."

Bella started to interrupt, but Owen held up his hand. "Let me finish. Please. I'll even show you the numbers, but I can lease it to you for the same amount you paid for your shop now. It's a Victorian house with a large front porch. Lots of room for your shop. Lots of windows, lots of light. It has an old carriage house behind it that has been converted into a small cottage to live in. Three bedrooms, two baths, and a small kitchen. A nice sunroom in the back. It has a fenced backyard the boys could play in."

"Owen, I can't let you do that."

"I've already bought the two houses. I'm keen on developing that area to help with the overall growth of the town. I have two tentative renters for the second building. I'm going to rent out both buildings whether you accept my offer and rent from me or not."

Bella sat silent for a moment. It seemed too good to be true. It would be a move of one block, right on the corner of Main Street and Rosewood. The area was developing quickly. She just didn't want to be a charity case for Owen. She'd built the shop up on her own. She didn't want him to give her a handout.

"Bella, dear, I think you should take Owen up on his offer. Sometimes it's hard to accept help, I know that. But Owen is a good man. I let him *give* us the building for my restaurant. I'll tell you why he did that too." Sylvia turned to her son. "It's time the truth came out."

Jake nodded to his mother.

Sylvia sat down in the chair beside Bella while Jake leaned against the porch railing. "You see, Owen's father is also Jake's father. He never acknowledged Jake or did anything to help raise him. Owen recently found out and came looking for Jake. Then he bought the building that had been my grandparents' —the one I had my restaurant in before I got sick. So much of my family history is in those walls. So many memories. And I loved running the restaurant there. Owen gave the building back to us, no strings attached. I'm a proud woman, but not too proud to take help for something I really want. Owen felt his father owed us this much."

Bella looked at Owen. She had judged him so harshly, thinking it was all just a cold business deal. But it wasn't. Owen was trying to do right by his brother. He was an honorable man, and she was a judging fool. "Owen, why didn't you tell me?"

"That would be my fault. I asked him not to tell anyone. Didn't want people talking about Mama again. But you know, I'm kind of glad the secret is out. It's not all bad having a brother." Jake reached out his hand to Owen.

Bella watched as boyish grin spread across Owen's face.

Owen jumped up and shook his brother's hand. "No, it's not a bad thing having a brother."

"So, you see, Bella. You'd be putting my mind at ease if you accepted Owen's offer. I wouldn't feel so badly about you losing your space for your shop and your place to live with your boys." Sylvia looked at Bella expectantly.

Owen turned to Bella. "I can see your mind churning. I'll show you my figures to prove I'm still turning a profit when I rent to you. It's not a handout, it's a business deal. This should also solve the problem of Rick insisting he's going to take the boys away. No judge is going to give him custody because you moved one block. One block closer to their school, too."

Bella's mind whirled. This would solve the problem with Rick and take away her fear that he'd get custody of the boys. That was her biggest problem right now. This solved it. And if it gave them a place to live along with a place for her shop, all her problems would be solved.

"I'd need to see the numbers. I don't want to be a charity case."

He reached into his notebook and gave her a typed-up page of numbers. She studied the figures for a few minutes. It did look like he was still making a profit. Not a great one, but a reasonable one. She looked up at Owen.

"I'd also like you to deal with the rental of the other house. I'm also looking for one more property on that street. If I find it I'd like you to manage it too. See if you can find renters for the rest of the office or shop space. If you could manage the properties for me, since I won't be in town all the time, it would really help me out," Owen said.

Yet another reason she should take the deal. She would be helping him out. Owen had thought of everything. No wonder he was known as a master dealmaker.

"I could have the lease ready to sign tomorrow." A hopeful expression crossed Owen's face. "I know you want to make it on your own. You still will be... with just a slight change of address. I do feel responsible for the upheaval I've caused in your life. Please let me do this one thing to try and make things right."

Bella was tempted. Very tempted. While her normal instinct was to say no, she'd find a place on her own, do it all on her own... this really was a good solution to her problems, especially to Rick's threat to take the boys away. She couldn't really think of a reason to say no except for her stubborn pride. Which was a really silly reason to turn this down.

"Well, you did cause all these problems." She flashed him a small smile.

Owen reached out and took her hand in his. "I think you'll love the building. Lots of windows. Great light. A handful of rooms on the ground floor to use for the shop and the second floor could be used for the shop too. A good sized yard for the boys. The house is empty now so you could move into it at anytime. I've already arranged for a cleaning service to clean it tomorrow. Like I said, I plan to rent to you if you want it, or to someone else if you don't. I'm committed to helping Comfort Crossing prosper."

It almost sounded too good to be true. She squeezed his hand. "I can't thank you enough for doing this."

"Is that a yes?"

"That is a yes. And a thank you."

Owen sat there with relief plainly evident on his face. She realized he'd been scared of her answer. Afraid he wouldn't be able to set right what he had caused when he bought the building the shop was in now.

"Oh, I'm so pleased." Sylvia clapped her hands. "Everything is going to work out for all of us, I just know it."

Owen took Bella's hand. "You think you could repay me by letting me kiss you again?"

Jake laughed out loud at his brother. "Real subtle."

Bella laughed, too. "You did all this for a kiss?"

"That and a chance to take you out on a date again." He flashed a wicked smile at her. "I'll have to be around a lot more now, what with having all these properties in town."

"And a brother. Don't forget you'll have a brother here," Jake said.

"That I will."

Bella looked over towards Owen, staring at those lips of his, the ones she'd wanted to kiss ever since the picnic.

Owen angled close and kissed her, his hand coming up to touch her face. The kiss rocked her world. So gentle but it pulled her deep into its emotional depths. Gave her hope for the future. A desire to get to know Owen better. A need, deep inside her, that she'd hidden for so long, began to beg her to be let free.

Jake cleared his throat.

She reluctantly pulled away from the kiss. Owen pulled her to her feet and wrapped his arms around her, holding her close.

Just then she heard voices coming from inside. She pulled away quickly, but Owen still held her hand clasped firmly in his.

"Hey, Momma. We brought you and Mr. Campbell some cookies." Timmy carefully made his way through the door with a plate of cookies balanced precariously in his hands. Jeremy and Rebecca followed in his wake.

"I love cookies," Owen said.

"Me, too." Bella smiled at her son as he put the plate of cookies on the table. "You boys know Ms. Landry and Jake, don't you?"

"Yep." Timmy said.

Jeremy nodded.

"Hello boys. That was nice of you to bring out cookies." Sylvia smiled at the boys.

Bella turned to her boys. "What do you guys say about going to see a new place for my shop and a new place to live?"

191

"Really?" Timmy beamed. "See, I told you if I could just talk to Mr. Campbell he could fix things." Timmy rushed over and wrapped his arms around Owen's waist. Bella could see that Owen was briefly taken aback by the unfamiliar hug from a child, but he dropped his arm to encircle Timmy.

"So we can still live with you?" Jeremy asked.

"I'm sure you can. It's only a block away from where we live now. It's on Rosewood Avenue. We can move in whenever we want."

"Man, Uncle Gil is going to be sad that we're not going to live with him," Timmy said.

Bella wasn't sure that was true. Her brother loved her boys, but living with them would probably have been more than her confirmed bachelor brother could have handled for long. "Well, Uncle Gil can visit you any time he wants."

"You two want to tag along and see the place?" Owen asked Jake and Sylvia.

"We sure would." Sylvia stood up.

"You boys want to go see it now? I have the keys." Owen held out the keys in front of him and smiled at Bella. A smile that warmed her and held a promise of things to come. Of time together getting to know each other. Of more of his fabulous, soul-shaking kisses.

Bella slipped her hand in Owen's and held tightly. "Come on boys. Let's go see the new shop and our new home. Everything is going to be just fine now."

Owen squeezed her hand and flashed that dashing smile of his at her. She finally believed her life might be falling perfectly into place.

Chapter Fifteen

Owen stood in Bella's backyard in a new pair of shorts and a t-shirt he'd bought yesterday. Casual shorts with cargo pockets and the t-shirt said Comfort Crossing— Best Small Town In Mississippi. He was positive he'd never had a t-shirt with a saying on it in his entire life.

They'd just finished up moving Bella's store and personal things into her new place. Jake had gotten a couple of his cousins to help. Sylvia had brought over enough food to feed an army. Jake and Gil were barbecuing burgers for the crowd of helpers.

A smattering of kids were running around the yard as well as a bunch of dogs. Jake's family always seemed to be accompanied by a large number of dogs. He watched while Timmy played fetch with one of the dogs, tossing a stick for the large collie-ish looking dog.

"Come on, boy. Come on. Bring me the stick." Timmy called to the pup. The dog obediently brought him the stick and Timmy tossed it again.

Sylvia came over and handed Owen a beer. "So, I just want you to know. Any brother of Jake's is a son to me. You're part of our family now."

Owen reached for the beer that Sylvia held out to him. He choked back the rush of emotions running through him. "I don't know what to say."

Sylvia smiled at him. "You might be sorry. We're kind of a big bunch of noisy bedlam."

"You're very kind to me, considering what my father did to you and Jake."

"That has nothing to do with you. He made his choices, and you've made yours. You've been very generous to us. I want you to know how much I appreciate it. I hope that you and Jake can become friends."

"I hope so too."

One of Jake's cousins came over and held out his hand. Owen thought his name was Spencer, but there were so many names to learn. "So, Jake told us you're his brother. Good for him. Always thought he could use a sibling. Anyway, welcome to the family."

"Thank you." Owen shook the man's hand. A family. He was part of Jake's family now. In a strange way, this was more his family than he'd ever felt with his mother and father.

"So how about you put that beer down and help me wrangle up these boys for a game of wiffle ball? Gotta tire my boys out. A tired boy is a good boy," Spencer said.

At least Owen thought it was Spencer. He was going to have to write all their names down and who went with whom.

"Go on. I'm going to finish setting out the food." Sylvia nodded towards the gaggle of boys playing in the yard.

Owen crossed the yard and got a game of wiffle ball going. There was good natured teasing and laughing going between the boys and the men. He tried to tag Jeremy out at home, but Jeremy plowed into him, knocking him down in the dirt.

Jeremy looked worried. "You, okay?"

"I'm fine. I better learn to get out of the way of the runner, shouldn't I?"

Jeremy grinned. "Yep."

Spencer reached a hand down to help him up. "Gotta be quick on your feet with this group."

Owen stood up and dusted the dirt off. He was having the time of his life at this backyard get-together, tumbles into the dirt and all. He looked up toward the house and saw Bella looking out the window and laughing. He waved to her and grinned.

* * * * *

Jenny watched as Izzy laughed and turned from the window. She came over and joined her friends in the sunroom. Becky Lee had unpacked the whole kitchen—Becky Lee insisted that she knew where everything should logically go. They had all agreed. Who was Izzy to argue with an accomplished cook?

Jenny had put the boys' things away in their closets. Izzy had repeatedly interrupted the unpacking to regale them with decorating plans for the house. Jenny was sure Izzy would take advantage of the light from every window. Every nook and cranny of the converted carriage house would be exploited.

The three friends sat on the couch, surrounded by more boxes they were ignoring, and sipped on some lemonade.

"I'm so glad school is over for the year and I could help you move." Jenny put her tired feet up on a box. "I love summers."

"They seem to go by too quickly though, don't they?" Izzy tugged a box nearer and put her feet up on it, too.

"Time does go by so fast, doesn't it? It seems like just yesterday Jenny had Nathan. He was this cute little toddler, just knee high to a grasshopper—I swear it was just last week. Now look at him. He's driving." Becky Lee sipped her lemonade.

The friends looked at each other. It had been a long time. They'd gone through a lot together. They knew things about each other that only the three of them knew.

Jenny sat staring at her lemonade, lost in her own thoughts. She'd had a lot to deal with this year with the loss of her husband and trouble with Nathan. She hoped the summer would be a relaxing one, but she had her doubts.

Jenny looked at her two friends and felt her heart warm with gratitude and love for them. She didn't know how she would have made it through her bumpy life without them along for the ride, supporting her, keeping her secrets.

"So are you going to see Owen again soon?" Becky Lee's question to Izzy brought Jenny out of her thoughts.

"I have a date with him tomorrow." Izzy grinned. "You know, if I can find something to wear."

"I reckon we could help you with that." Becky Lee said.

"Looks like he's redeemed himself." Jenny joined in.

Izzy smiled. "I think he has. I'm glad to see Jake and Owen become friends. It looks like Sylvia has practically adopted him as one of her own."

"About time you found someone to date who we approve of." Becky Lee grinned at her friend and raised her glass of lemonade. "To a bright future for our Izzy."

"I'll drink to that." Izzy raised her glass.

Jenny raised her lemonade and the three women clinked their glasses together. "To the best friends ever."

THANK YOU for reading *The Shop on Main*. I hope you enjoyed it. Learn more about my books and sign up for my newsletter to be updated with information on new releases, promotions, and give-aways at my website, kaycorrell.com

Reviews help other readers find new books. I'd appreciate it if you would leave an honest review.

Comfort Crossing ~ The Series

The Shop on Main - Book One
The Memory Box - Book Two
The Christmas Cottage - A Holiday Novella (Book 2.5)
The Letter - Book Three
The Christmas Scarf - A Holiday Novella (Book 3.5)
The Magnolia Cafe - Book Four
The Unexpected Wedding - Book Five (Summer of 2016)

The books are all part of a series, but each book can be read as a stand-alone story. Jenny and her best friends, Bella and Becky Lee, navigate the heartaches and triumphs of love and life in the small Southern town of Comfort Crossing, Mississippi

The Memory Box - Book Two
Sometimes, mistakes are made for the best of reasons...

When Dr. Clay Miller returns to Comfort Crossing with his two daughters, Jenny Bouchard knows it is time. Time to tell him the truth, no matter the consequences. Clay has a son, Nathan.

From the moment Jenny and Clay see each other again, the attraction still pulsates between them, a fact they both do their best to ignore. Jenny searches for the right moment to tell Clay the truth and a chance to explain—she had made her choice, kept her secret, to protect her son. When Nathan is injured, she knows her time is running out. Jenny fears when the truth is revealed, she will lose not only Clay, but Nathan as well.

But Clay has a secret of his own...

The Christmas Cottage - A Novella (Book 2.5)
A story of love, moving on, and a dog name Louie...

Veterinarian Holly Thompson accepts a temporary position in Comfort Crossing in an effort to escape all things Christmas. What she finds is a small town that embraces all things Christmas and a handsome neighbor with a small son who both capture her heart. Add to that their adorable pup, and she knows the holidays are not going to be what she planned. At all.

Steve Bergeron is quite content being a single father. He's not willing to risk his heart — or his son's — on another woman who is sure to leave them. It's quite clear Holly will be gone by the new year. But he finds himself willing to do anything to chase away the sadness that lurks in the depths of Holly's eyes. This isn't part of his carefully laid out plans. At all.

When an accident on Christmas Eve forces them both to question their choices, can the magic of the season warm their hearts and bring love and joy back into their lives?

The Letter ~ Book Three
Sometimes life offers second chances …

Madeline Stuart, a St. Louis-based accountant, has sworn off relationships. Reeling from a breakup with her long-term boyfriend and her mother's recent death, she's determined to avoid personal entanglements of any kind.

Deserted by his big-city girlfriend because he's a "country bumpkin," Gil Amaud, a business owner in Comfort Crossing, Mississippi, has sworn off women.

Madeline's curiosity is piqued when she finds an old letter hidden in her grandmother's antique writing desk addressed to Josephine Amaud in Comfort Crossing.

With Gil's help, she tracks Josephine down and learns the letter is from her first beau, who disappeared suddenly many years ago.
While they search for Josephine's lost love, both Gil and Madeline try to deny the attraction developing between them.

Can a big-city woman and a small-town businessman help to reunite the star-crossed lovers? And can they find a way to put aside their differences to build a future together in this sweet, heartwarming tale of love and forgiveness?

Maybe, just maybe, a second chance is all they really need.

The Christmas Scarf ~ A Holiday Novella (Book 3.5)

Sometimes, Christmas wishes bring their own special magic...

A woman chasing a life-long dream. A man given a second chance at love. If one wins, the other loses. Does a stranger's scarf hold enough magic to make both their Christmas wishes come true?

Missy Sherwood has always wished for one thing, to be a country singer. After trying to make it for years in Nashville, she returns to her hometown of Comfort Crossing, Mississippi, feeling like a misfit and a failure.

But there's no use in telling anyone the truth just yet—she's here for longer than the holidays, she's home for good. Right?

Dylan Rivers is glad to see his old friend return to town, not only to help him with the children's Christmas pageant, but because her homecoming sparks long-forgotten but never acted upon feelings. But there is no use in acting on those feelings, she's soon to head back to her fabulous career in Nashville. Right?

Then a stranger comes to town and has Missy re-examining her dreams. She gets one final chance, and her life-long wish is within her grasp. Is there really magic in the stranger's scarf, or is it in the power of knowing her heart's true wish?

The Magnolia Cafe ~ Book Four

Sometimes, the past isn't quite what it seems…

Reluctant restauranteur, Keely Granger, wants nothing more than to escape the small town she's lived in her whole life, but her guilt and family responsibilities keep her firmly entrenched in Comfort Crossing, Mississippi.

Lonely photojournalist, Hunt Robichaux, takes a break from his life-is-short, chase-after-your-dreams lifestyle and returns home to help his recently widowed sister and his nephews. But every responsibility he's ever taken on ends in disaster, so he's determined to leave before anyone starts to depend on him.

As Keely and Hunt's relationship develops into a more-than-childhood-friends level, Hunt has to decide if he's been chasing his dreams in the wrong part of the world. But as secrets from their past begin to unravel, Keely reels from the knowledge that everything she's believed to be true is all a lie. A disaster — and the truth — threaten to tear them apart forever.

The Unexpected Wedding ~ Book Five (summer of 2016)

Kay Correll writes stories that are a cross between contemporary romance and women's fiction. She likes her fiction with a healthy dose of happily ever after. Her stories are set in the fictional small town of Comfort Crossing, Mississippi. While her books are a series, each one can be read as a stand-alone story.

Kay lives in Missouri and can often be found out and about with her camera, taking a myriad of photographs which she likes to incorporate into her book covers. When not lost in her writing or photography, she can be found spending time with her ever-supportive husband, working in her garden, or playing with her puppies—two cavaliers and one naughty but adorable Australian shepherd. Kay and her husband also love to travel. When it comes to vacation time, she is torn between a nice trip to the beach or the mountains—but the mountains only get considered in the summer—she swears she's allergic to snow.

Learn more about Kay and her books at kaycorrell.com While there, be sure to sign up for her newsletter to hear about new releases, sales, and giveaways.